The Fracking King

The FRACKING KING

A NOVEL

James Browning

NEW HARVEST
HOUGHTON MIFFLIN HARCOURT
2014

This edition published by special arrangement with Amazon Publishing

Amazon and the Amazon logo are trademarks of Amazon.com, Inc., or its affiliates.

For information about permission to reproduce selections from this book, go to www.apub.com.

www.hmhco.com

Library of Congress Cataloging-in-Publication Data
Browning, James (Environmentalist)
The fracking king : a novel / James Browning.
page   cm
ISBN 978-0-544-26299-7 (hardback)
1. Gifted persons – Fiction. 2. Scrabble (Game) – Fiction. 3. Competition – Fiction.
4. Ecology – Fiction. 5. Psychological fiction. I. Title.
PS3602.R7377F73 2014
813'.6 – dc23
2013045485

Printed in the United States of America
DOC 10 9 8 7 6 5 4 3 2 1

Love

A tender feeling
Or the object of such a feeling
Or a love affair
Or a score of zero (as in tennis).

— Thomas Urlacher

Part One

1

The first person I ever saw light Fitler's water on fire was my old roommate Rich. The sight of flaming tap water scared the hell out of me but Rich was from Ohio and had seen whole rivers burn.

Like many great discoveries at our sad, cold boarding school in northeastern Pennsylvania, Rich made his by accident. He was smoking by the sink when the water burst into flames and an orange fireball shot up to the ceiling. In a flash, I thought about all the times I'd seen my friend fall asleep with a lit cigarette in his mouth. The time he stubbed one out but, then, flicked it out the window at a gas station. I won't say it made sense that he could light water on fire. But I felt this must be it and that the fearless, foolish Richard Urlacher would finally be burned alive.

2

dude we r gonna rock this thing c u soon Richard Urlacher

It's my fault that I got this message three months late. Too late to ask the Hale School for a different roommate. I got my own phone in June—a Jitterbug designed for senior citizens—and spent the summer feeling bad that no one had called me. Finally, I called the phone company and was told that all my calls and messages were going to a man named Crow.

My name is Winston Crwth and most people called me Win. The Crwths came to America from Wales a long time ago and most had the good sense to change their name to Crowther, Crow, or McWhorter. Crwth was so ugly that people assumed it must be a typo. Teachers who knew how to say things like "prix fixe" or "!Kung" would stare at Crwth, shake their heads, and ask me to say my name.

"Crwth," I'd say, "it rhymes with 'truth.'"

"Oh, so with a *u*?"

"No, it's with a *w*."

I straightened things out with the phone company and was sitting in the car when I got Richard's text. (My father was driving me to Hale for the start of my junior year, and my phone was almost drained from searching for a signal in the Endless Mountains.) I had been hazed at each of my last two schools—the thugs at Hannah Penn making fun of me for using "Scrabble words," and the flakes at Clovis Friends publishing my Scrabble words in the school newspaper as if they were poetry—and now had a bad feeling that I would be hazed with rocks. Hale was in coal country and had just leased a lot of its land to Dark Oil & Gas. A school whose existence had always been precarious had suddenly struck it rich and had given me one of their new Dark Scholarships. Dark "fracked" for natural gas in the hills above the Hale School, and while I didn't really know what fracking was, I knew it involved drilling through a mile or more of rock.

3

"Don't worry," my father said. "Texting makes all young people sound like idiots."

"Dad, I don't know, you used to say the same thing about email."

"I did?"

"That email made Mom sound mad at you."

"No, that was the phone," he said.

My parents got divorced when I was six years old. Since then I had been living with my father in Philadelphia during the school year and spending my summers with my mother in San Francisco. My parents met at a Scrabble tournament, and sometimes it seemed like this word game was the only thing a friendly kid from Philly and a surly girl from Fog City had in common. Although, after their divorce, they both said the exact same thing about my suddenly fractured childhood — that growing up in Philadelphia and San Francisco would make me "cosmopolitan."

I did not know what this meant and was too ashamed to ask. Thanks to Scrabble I knew a lot of words for a six-year-old, almost all of which had eight letters or less. (You get seven tiles at a time in Scrabble and words with more than eight are rare.) As a kid I loved the game because playing meant that my parents would not fight — or not fight with each other. Instead they would curse the Q or vilify the I or talk trash about Noah Webster himself for arbitrarily removing the u from words like "colour" and "humour" to make them more American. After their divorce I played in my room, against myself, because it was too painful to play against my parents anymore. I would read their words for some clue to what they'd done; and while I knew better than to take their words literally, I began to cry when my mother turned WIN into TWIN, as if she wished there were two of me and she could take one of us to California. Maybe it's true that an infinite number of monkeys typing on an infinite number of keyboards will eventually produce the complete works of Shakespeare. But you'd go mad reading all of their rough drafts, just as you'd go mad reading Scrabble as if the words have meaning.

Hale would be my third high school in the last three years and I was beginning to wonder if, instead of cosmopolitan, I was just a well-traveled fool. As a freshman, I went to the public school where my father taught U.S. history. Hannah Penn High smelled like a tuna fish sandwich and had a fiendish boiler that made the air so hot, so dry, that kids got nosebleeds and walked around with tissues crammed into their nostrils as if they'd all been in fights. I drank coffee and lay low with my father in the faculty lounge, and was doing fine until an older kid threatened to cut my tongue out if I used any more "Scrabble words" around his girlfriend. All I'd done was say "cwm," which means "a valley in Wales," but the kid thought it was some obscure part of his girlfriend's anatomy.

After this, my father got a second mortgage on our house so I could go to Clovis Friends, a Quaker school just north of Philadelphia. Clovis had a café instead of a cafeteria and served coffee its own students grew on trips to Costa Rica. Kids called teachers by their first names. I became the captain of their Scrabble "team." Clovis Friends was one of just a few high schools in Pennsylvania with its own interscholastic Scrabble team — the Hale School for Boys was another one — but I put "team" in quotes because while these kids knew all the two-letter words, things like "aa" and "oe," many did not believe in keeping score, or sticking to the rules and might just walk away in the middle of a game. Or they used their tiles to write dirty poetry, or play a kind of linguistic Twister in which they had to

or attempt other things that were anatomically impossible. Hannah Penn was rough but Clovis Friends was not rough enough, and I hoped with Hale that I was finally going to get it right.

"Maybe writing on his phone makes Richard sound like an idiot," my father said. "Or maybe he really is an idiot. Girls all love his dad but I've never liked his stuff."

"Stuff?" I said.

"His father is the PA poet laureate."

"The what?" I said, even as the name Thomas Urlacher came to me. Urlacher was famous for copying several definitions of love from a dictionary, then writing "Love" over them and calling this a poem. Lots of kids at Clovis Friends seemed to read his stuff and some could recite his stuff, so I decided that Richard Urlacher might not be such an idiot.

"Thomas is the poet laureate of Pennsylvania. You know, it's like I have two kinds of students now. Kids who write their home-work and thought papers on their phones. Kids who just sound like they do."

My father taught five sections of U.S. history at Hannah Penn, 160 kids in all, and refused to give tests or pop quizzes, meaning he had 160 "thought papers" to grade each weekend. Besides history, my father loved the Phillies and shooting pool and once told me that "the only way to make a shot is, first, to miss it in every way possible." A tragic philosophy that I thought explained his life. Before getting his master's degree in U.S. history, he actually spent several years trying to get a Ph.D. in SoFoPo, or Soviet foreign policy, only to have the Soviet Union suddenly go belly-up. He switched to U.S. history and was doing fine until the Internet came along. He had always loved to be the first person to cut the pages in a book, or put on cotton gloves to handle certain books as if they were bones or fossils that might crumble at his touch. A pile of rotten red blocks that had been sitting in a corner of our base-ment for as long as I could remember had turned out to be *The New Soviet Encyclopedia* — a gluey monstrosity that my father got in Leningrad in 1985 in exchange for the Walkman off his ears and the Nikes off his feet. He loved books, but now you could know anything about anyone in history with the click of a mouse or a tap of your finger. Or so my father feared. My mother tried to tell him that these two things — the collapse of the Soviet Union and the rise of the Internet — were not mistakes but just bad luck, and that books, newspapers, magazines, and the printed word were not going to disappear. But he did not believe her.

I was luckier than my father as the great love of my life seemed to be indestructible. I played Scrabble with tiles as a kid and now played online against people from all around the world, although players outside the U.S. and Canada use a much bigger dictionary — so big that the whole thing starts to seem ridiculous. Kids at Hannah Penn and even kids at Clovis Friends made fun of me for playing words like "zebrass," a sterile cross between a zebra and an ass, as if my lousy social life had driven me to study other strange creatures that could never reproduce. But even I drew the line at "zo," a cross between a Tibetan yak and a Tibetan cow, in part because "zo" makes it too easy to get rid of the Z.

4

The drive from Philadelphia seemed to be uphill all the way — up the Schuylkill Valley and up into the foothills of the Endless Mountains in northeastern Pennsylvania. Hale was founded in 1890, right after the Johnstown Flood. You could even say Hale was founded because of the flood. I had known this ever since Hale offered me a scholarship and my father told me to "look before you leap." As a freshman, I leaped into Hannah Penn before reading about her marriage to the much older William Penn and did not understand when a senior put her arm around me and asked if I wanted to "pull a Penn" on her. The girl had a tattoo of an octopus on her wrist, and I worried that I was now supposed to draw on her. Only later did I learn that she was asking me on a date and that "pull a Penn" meant to honor Hannah Penn by dating someone much older.

I made a bigger mistake when I leaped at the chance to get the hell out of Hannah Penn and go to Clovis Friends. My father told me that Clovis was for gifted kids and that the school would appreciate my unique abilities. But what he didn't say was that Clovis Smith was the only man known to have been elected to Congress without knowing how to read. Smith could recite whole books of the Bible from memory and give entire speeches without a stumble or an "um." But the words in books "swam before his eyes" and gave Smith vertigo. Like William Penn, Smith married a much younger Quaker and the two of them founded a school for boys who were in some way "afflicted," most of them physically, though some shared Smith's curse of words that swam before their eyes. Old photographs of Clovis graduates show many of them in wheelchairs or wearing braces to help them cope with polio. More recent photos show boys and girls staring into space or staring fixedly at something on their phones.

I would not get fooled again. Hale's brochure said the school was founded as a "kinder, gentler" alternative to other Pennsylvania boarding schools, a place where boys would be taught to think for themselves and be given a measure of freedom because "freedom teaches responsibility." Kinder, gentler wasn't hard, at first, as many schools in the nineteenth century were little more than farms or factories where, after a long day of plowing the fields or trying to pick cotton out of the jennies without getting their fingers smashed, boys were taught to read and write. Instead of manual labor, Hale had its students go to class on Saturdays — a kinder, gentler approach to education that had endured beyond the passage of child labor laws and the rise of the "weekend," so that Hale and a few military academies were now crueler, harder as the only schools in Pennsylvania to have classes on Saturdays. I read online that a Hale student had killed himself a few years ago and that many students and teachers blamed Hale's schedule—classes in the morning, afternoon, and night, classes on Saturdays, some optional classes for students who could not afford to travel home for the holidays. But instead of cutting back on work, the school responded to this tragedy by lifting its 118-year-old ban on boys having girls in their rooms. Now a boy could have a girl in his room between 6 P.M. and 8 P.M. if he got his housemaster's permission, if the door was kept open, and if boy and girl kept a total of "three feet on the floor." My chances of finding a girlfriend at a school for boys seemed about as good as drawing RR—a tile that only appears in Spanish versions of Scrabble, and which only wound up in my bag once by mistake—but this new rule thrilled me.

Elijah Hale would say that he founded Hale to advance the idea that "children have souls." But it is also true that helping children was plan B. He originally bought the land so he could build a dam and create a "lake in the sky" and have "sailboats in the mountains," just like they did at Lake Conemaugh—the lake above Johnstown where Hale and many other wealthy Pennsylvania families had summer cottages. Hale had dammed the Skulking River and was laying railroad tracks when he got the news that Conemaugh's dam had burst and more than two thousand people had been killed in the resulting flood, fires, and mayhem. A plateau in the foothills of the Endless Mountains was not a great place for a boarding school, either, but that's what became of the lodge, the cottages, and the few houses that Hale had already built; and with its small endowment and the gradual collapse of most industries in northeastern Pennsylvania—steel, lumber, coal, and the railroads on which these things had been shipped—the school had struggled for most of its history.

5

Fitler Hall was the darkest, most Dickensian dorm at Hale. I could tell this just by looking at a photograph, but I didn't know why it was so dark until we drove through Hale's gates and parked in the shadow of the Dreissegacker Natatorium, a building so big it had a dark side like a moon. The dark side of Dreissegacker was ten to fifteen degrees colder than the rest of Hale and could not support certain forms of life. Instead of fruit, a blueberry bush in front of Fitler grew little, wooden knobs. The grass near Fitler grew either spiky, short, and brown, or spiky, short, and a garish shade of green that was actually paint — the same shade of green as the grass that grew around the natural gas wells I'd seen driving up from Philadelphia. The things in the pots in my housemaster's windows were lumpy, stunted, and looked more like rocks than plants. Dr. Goltz was a geologist and I would learn later that he kept rocks in pots; at the time I worried that I, too, would wither in Dreissegacker's shadow.

Rich's and my room was on the second floor. A quick glance at Dreissegacker to the south, then a longer look at the Endless Mountains to the east and west, made me wonder if our room got direct sunlight. One of my father's students had gone to Yale and later told a wild story about a man who gave Yale a girls' dorm but stipulated that all of his descendants who went to Yale be given the penthouse suite — even if they were male. A dark dorm surrounded by grass that had been painted green made me think that Fitler was a trustee or a boy who had died and that his family would not let Hale knock Fitler down.

Fitler looked so grim and the air felt so cold that I panicked and produced the first text message of my life.

who was Fitler?

I pushed Send. My phone thwipped as if my free throw had hit nothing but net. I needed to know more about Hale and really needed to know if I'd be living with an idiot, and here was a way to kill two birds with one stone. Rich wrote back to me at once.

> dude I'm at the Contraceptive Variety Store in town do u
> > need anything
> the what?
> the CVS
> no but I am wondering who was Fitler?

It took all my self-control not to start my sentences with a capital letter, but this was how Rich wrote and I didn't want my roommate to think I was a dork.

> Fitler was a guy whose name rhymed with Hitler is that
> > no on condoms
> yes

6

My dad parked on the grass and said, "Win, I am so proud of you."

"Thanks, Dad, that means a lot. Any last words of advice?"

"How about what my father said when I switched from Soviet to U.S. history? 'Son, you don't know what you're doing, so just be confident as hell.'"

I laughed. My grandfather was a mean old man who smoked and lived alone in Harrisburg and was still dating in his late eighties, in part because he had a car and still had his license. After my grandmother died, he had married one of his old college sweethearts. She died, too, and while my grandfather didn't mean to propose marriage to every surviving female member of his college class, that is how his letter seeking companionship read, and one of these women was about to marry him when my father intervened and drove her back to Ohio.

Elijah Hale never got to build his "lake in the sky," but the Dreissegacker Natatorium had to be the next best thing — a huge building that held the school's swimming pool and its ice hockey rink. Dreissegacker looked like an art gallery from the front, with glass walls and a cresting glass roof that looked like a frozen wave. From back here it was all brick and smokestacks and could have been a public high school or a factory. Life on the dark side seemed sadder, grayer, than life on the bright. The trees were stunted, spindly, and their leaves were orange and brown. The grass was either brown or the bright green color which was clearly paint.

A boy sitting on a bench was shivering and pulling his sweatshirt around his chest, his hood tight around his head until he looked like a monk.

"Rich?" I said.

The boy shook his head. "Rich is at CVS."

"Winston Crwth," I said, and held out my hand.

"Crwth like truth?" he said, and shook my hand without looking up from his phone.

"Uh-huh."

"So with a *u*?" he said.

"No, it's with a *w*."

"Charles Hosefros," he said. "Though Rich calls me Frozen Hose."

"Why does Rich call you that?"

"I get shy around girl."

"Don't you mean around 'girls'?"

Hose pushed back his hood and I saw his crew cut and a small tattoo behind his ear — a brownish rectangle that looked like a rusty window or the blank tile in Scrabble. "No, I mean I get shy around Thomasina Wodtke-Weir."

"Who is she?"

"The only girl at the Hale School for Boys."

"No way."

"Her father is the headmaster and he sends his daughter here. Hey, Win, can I come over sometime when she's in your room?"

It's amazing how many people feel sorry for me because of my last name and guess correctly that my nickname is Win. My name starts out fine but jumps the tracks and turns into a wreck — a "madhouse of consonants," to quote one of my father's favorite novelists — and becomes a lesson on what to do with ugliness.

My last girlfriend had been in junior high. Stacy Yant sat next to me at lunch because she liked the sound of my voice. Stacy talked as if she had just burned her tongue and pronounced the letter *t* as *d* a lot — Winston Crwth became Windom Crude — and I never knew why until she popped the pink clam of her retainer out and wrapped it in a napkin. One day Stacy took my hand and led me behind the cafeteria in a way that made my friends think I was some kind of Don Juan . . . and some kind of weirdo when I came back reeking of fish, sour milk, and mayonnaise. Everyone assumed that we had been making out. Really, we climbed in a dumpster and went through more than a hundred bags of trash before finding the napkin that held her retainer.

"And I'll have girls in my room because . . . ?"

"Girl."

"Girl in my room because . . ." — I didn't want to say the words for fear of making them true — "because she and Rich are . . . ?"

"That's what we all want to know. She's the first girl in the history of the school to be in a boy's room legally."

"With Rich?"

Hose shook his head like someone trying to get a drop of water out of his ear. "She also had a thing for the editor of the school newspaper. Although Thomasina was, like, twelve or thirteen then and just living on campus, so I guess that's not the same as being a student here. Although she's been mistaken for a librarian because of her hair."

"What's wrong with her hair?"

"It's gray."

"All of it?"

"A lot."

"How much really?"

"Just a streak."

"Who was the guy before Rich?"

"Stephen Ha."

I am terrible with names and don't even listen when people introduce themselves. I can't blame all of my problems on Scrabble — though names and other proper nouns are not allowed and, therefore, not relevant — and Stacy Yant would say that I was a self-centered jerk. Still, I'd seen the name Stephen Ha but could not remember where.

"Who is Ha?" I asked.

"He's not . . . You wouldn't know . . . He's not here anymore. Ha was the second-best Scrabble player in Pennsylvania."

"So he, what, dropped out of school and turned professional?" I had written about my dream of going pro in my Hale application, though the Scrabble circuit offered so little prize money that only one man in America had ever made a living off the game. Carlos Gomez y Garcia had won the national championship at the age of fifteen and had been declared the Bobby Fischer of Scrabble. There is no such thing, of course, since chess is all skill and Scrabble takes a lot of luck, but, like Fischer, Gomez y Garcia railed against what he saw as corruption in his sport and withdrew from competition in his mid-twenties. Now he lived in Belize and was stalked by eager Scrabblers, the way young writers looked for J. D. Salinger's house in New Hampshire.

"No," Hose said, "Ha killed himself."

"Why?" I said.

"It's hard to say. He got straight sixes" — the Hale equivalent of an A — "and he was the editor of the school newspaper. He had a girlfriend back in New York and got into Yale early, so what's not to live for?"

"This was in the *Inky*."

"What?"

"The *Philadelphia Inquirer*. They said Ha didn't leave a note?"

"That's just it — he did," Hose said. "Ever hide under the sink or, like, under the bed as a kid?"

"I hid in a box," I said.

"Ha hid his note in plain sight. He was in the state championships in Harrisburg and it's like he lost interest and kept skipping his turn, or playing little, crazy words in one corner of the board. The guy he was playing must have weighed three-fifty and kept tapping his toes so that the whole board shook. Ha didn't notice and he didn't seem to care."

"Crazy how?"

"Like 'eye.'"

"Like 'I'?"

"Like e-y-ẹ for barely any points. Like 'want' when he could have played 'wanting' for a bingo and the fifty extra points. Do I have to spell it out?"

"I hate that word."

"'Bingo'?"

"They took the most beautiful thing about the game and gave it a name —"

"Never fails," Hose said, and sighed.

I thought Hose meant that I'd just said something profound—that ugly names blinded us to things that were beautiful all the time. I can be reading Keats, the *Inky*, the dictionary,
or texts by Richard Urlacher and miss the meaning because I'm
busy figuring out how many points each word would be worth in
Scrabble. Or I'll see my mother write something like "I love you"
in an email and I'll move the letters around until I've got "O evil
you." I had no idea why Ha played EYE and WANT until Hose
unfolded a board and played these chilling words for me:

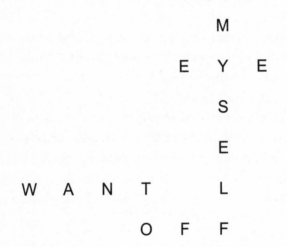

"And do you want to know what's even more amazing? Ha
didn't off himself until he'd won the game and gone back to his
hotel room. He wrote his suicide note in front of an audience and
no one even saw."

7

I walked back to my father's car, a black VW whose engine was
still crackling. I put my hand on the hood and it felt warm and

comforting—the best and perhaps the last source of heat near Fitler Hall. I checked my phone to see how Rich was doing at CVS. His trip sounded idiotic but the phrase "Contraceptive Variety" had captured my imagination and made it seem like Rich shared his father's gift for finding poetry where you'd least expect it.

My father stood still and dumb as a mule while I draped my bags on his shoulders and around his neck.

"I can't see."

I flattened a bag so he could see where he was going and his brow furrowed at the sight of Fitler Hall.

"This is where you're going to live? I knew these Dark Scholarships were too good to be true. What's that sound?"

I listened and heard a distant pounding sound.

"Construction?"

"No, it's something else."

"Fracking?"

"Challenge," my father said—a word that makes my face turn red as if I have been slapped. "Challenge" is what you say when your opponent plays or seems to play something that is not a word, and you want to call their bluff. Some parents spank their kids and some abuse them verbally. My father had challenged so many of my mistakes and childish bluffs—denouncing "erie" as a misspelling and, worse, a lie when I said, "No, it's a person or a thing embodying the qualities of Erie, Pennsylvania"—that I had a mortal fear of *saying* things that weren't words. And of course this was the point. My father and I had just spent several hours trying to figure out what fracking was, boggling at so much grass being painted green, or the kid we saw selling "frackwater" for fifty cents a glass as if it were lemonade. Fracking was everywhere in northeastern Pennsylvania—a future for a place that had been stuck in the past—but we had concluded that we didn't want to know. Dark Oil & Gas was paying for my education and that was enough. The fact that "frack" was not a word — my father had tried to look it up in the Scrabble dictionary — was actually very helpful and he knew that "challenge" would help me put it out of mind.

8

Fitler Hall was an old three-story Victorian and the steps creaked loudly as we walked up to the door. The floor inside creaked and sagged under my feet and was soon accompanied by a metal bonging sound as my father climbed the stairs. Rich and I had a room on the second floor, meaning we would live in Dreissegacker's shadow and might never see the sun. The floor of our room was made of a brown rubbery material which suggested that not all Hale students were toilet-trained. Rich's dirty shoes and socks were already strewn around the room and his cigarette butts littered the window sills. His pink shirts flocked in the closet like flamingos.

"Good luck," my father said, and hugged me and kissed me on the cheek. "Don't spend all your time playing Scrabble."

"Phtpht," I said.

"Tsktsk," he said. After "crwth," a Welsh fiddle that no one plays anymore, these are the two longest words that do not have a vowel.

I listened to him bonging down the stairs and driving away in his VW, a car that sounded like it was endlessly clearing its throat, and remembered what he said about learning to make a shot in pool by, first, missing it in every way possible. Hale had to be better than my first two high schools. And no matter how bad Rich and my dorm turned out to be, I was a Dark Scholar and the whole thing was free. Dark was even paying for my books and meals, and all they'd asked in return was that I attend a dinner with my fellow Dark Scholars from other schools in Pennsylvania — all of which had leased their land to Dark Oil & Gas.

Our room was stifling. It was just the second week of September but Fitler's radiators were on full blast, and Rich or someone had opened our windows to try to cool things down. The air in our room was hot and damp and cold at once, and made me feel as if I was getting the flu. Our beds were on either side of the hissing, spitting radiator. The damned thing even began to hum and moan intermittently, but this was the humming of Dr. Goltz, our housemaster, coming through the pipes.

I unpacked my things and went to the bathroom and came back to find Hose on the floor, his long arms and legs splayed out awkwardly. He looked like a marionette that had been flung down in disgust.

"Scrab?" he said.

"Sure thing," I said, and sat across from him.

"Winter rules or regular?"

"What are winter rules?" I said.

Hose blushed. "I thought you'd know. I mean Rich has been trying to call you and get in touch with you since the second we found out that you would be coming here."

"Why?"

"We thought you sounded like the hottest thing since Stephen Ha. Or I did. Rich was more concerned you were this giant loser."

"My phone calls were going to a man named Crow," I said.

"Dude, it's really cold in here. Why don't you close the window?"

"Why don't you?"

Hose rolled up his sleeve and showed me a long, thin scar that he said he got by falling asleep and flopping his arm across the radiator in his room. "They have two settings — hellishly hot or so cold that icicles form inside your windows."

I closed one window and saw that Rich or someone had run fishing line from a hook outside our other window to the branches of a tree. I tugged the line and something white popped out of a hole, as if I'd disturbed a nest. I tugged the line the other way but the thing would not go back.

"I'll have one of those," Hose said.

"One of what?"

"A cigarette."

I had disturbed Rich's hiding place and figured it was better to reel in his cigarettes than to leave them in plain sight.

"You don't smoke?" Hose said as I threw the cigarettes on Rich's bed. Our room had a fire escape and I saw two footprints in the dust on Rich's sill.

"I don't give away other people's property. Is it true what they say about 'two strikes'?" "Two strikes and you're out" was supposed to be Hale's rule for kids who committed major infractions like drinking, smoking, cheating, or sneaking out of the dorms at night.

"Kids whose fathers went here seem to get about three strikes. And kids whose fathers gave the school a swimming pool or a building, or whose families own hotels or the Mets or things like that, get five or six strikes before Hale finally kicks them out. Also, I doubt they'd expel the winner of a Dark Scholarship."

"No?"

"You guys are incredible. Jason Moskowitz can type, like, ninety words a minute without any mistakes. Stephen Ha read the dictionary from A to Z as if it was a book."

"I did that."

"Yeah, but can you speak three languages? Can you recite the first two acts of *The Tempest* from memory?"

"Ha was a Dark Scholar, too?" I didn't mind the sound of this

Moskowitz, but Ha sounded downright frightening. Not because he'd killed himself, but because his talents suggested real genius.

"Sure," Hose said, "Ha was one of the first."

"But there's only been fracking for a few years, right? Hale just leased its land to Dark —"

"There's been fracking in Texas and Oklahoma since the nineteen-fifties. That's how Dark knows it's safe," Hose said.

"Says who?"

"Says my dad," Rich said, walking into the room and throwing something small and gray at my chest — a slippery plastic package that I crammed into my pants. "One condom enough for you?"

"Probably more than enough."

9

Rich sat smoking in the windowsill while Hose and I finished our Scrabble game. Rich seemed bored and sighed and blew smoke out of his nose. He finished his cigarette and peeked nervously at my rack as if I was going to spell something important or something about him. Rich's shoes were resting on the radiator, and he got so absorbed in what I was doing that the heel on one shoe turned into gray chewing gum.

"Huh," Rich said, "I never knew there were so many words without vowels."

"You don't play?"

"I can barely read."

"Why can't you —"

"Dyslexia."

I used to feel sorry for people with dyslexia. One guy at Clovis Friends had to have all of his books and even his homework assignments put on CD or on his iPod so he could listen to them, and the only way to get through all of his homework was to speed these recordings up until he was listening to Thoreau, French, and algebra as read by Alvin and the Chipmunks. Then I saw the toll that Scrabble took on some of its top players. Many were so fat they hid their chairs and seemed to float above their boards. Others were so thin and pale, the purple bags under their eyes suggesting long, sleepless nights, or chronic feelings of guilt, that they could have died and you wouldn't know it till their time to play a word expired, too, and their clock began to buzz. I was considered a "looker" on the Scrabble circuit but I was young and hadn't wrecked my body or, for that matter, my mind for the sake of Scrabble yet.

"Rich, what did you mean when you said that you and I were going to 'rock' this place?"

Rich laughed. "I don't remember saying that, but it sounds like me. Probably just being friendly. Or maybe I wanted to make sure you wouldn't try to steal my girl like Frozen Hose. Hose, you can go home, you know. Thomasina won't be coming here tonight. She might not come all fall now that I've got a roommate."

"You've been living alone?" I said.

"My old roommate got kicked out for cruising. And not even for a girl. Doug was a photographer for the school newspaper and got kicked out for taking pictures of some gunk."

"Fracking gunk?"

"Uh-huh," he said.

"Is there some kind of rule that you can't write about fracking?"

"No," Rich said, "the dummy shot the moon in the background so that Dr. Goltz could tell he'd been out after sign-in."

"So one strike and he was out?"

Rich shook his head. "Doug's first strike was for smoking.

Goltz went nuts. Goltz *knows* I smoke, but he's, like, obsessed with kids not doing it in the second-floor bathroom."

"So Goltz hates the smell?" I said.

"Goltz hates the smell and his wife hates the fact that you can hear everything going on in their apartment through the pipes. That's my guess. Because the reason Goltz gave Doug — that smoking in the bathroom was somehow *dangerous* — doesn't make any sense."

I'd signed up for Rocks for Jocks — officially known as Introduction to Geology — because it was supposed to be the cakewalk of the science department, and because I wanted something to talk about in my thank-you letters to Ian and Trevonia Dark, the people who gave me my Dark Scholarship. I had been a good student and did well on standardized tests, but was still amazed that I got a scholarship. And while I liked the sound of fracking less and less — couldn't fracking near the school turn it into Centralia, the hollowed-out Pennsylvania town where an underground coal fire had been burning since my father was a kid? — "aa" and "pahoehoe" and other names for rocks were also some of my favorite words and so I thought the class might be good for Scrabble, too.

"Where's Doug now?"

"In Leah."

"Where?"

"The massively multiplayer online role-playing game that recreates the boarding school experience. Doug and the rest of the staff of the *Hale Mountaineer*."

"They all got kicked out?" I said.

"No, they meet in Leah now because, I mean, there's no *paper* and no reason for them to be in the same place physically."

"Do you play?"

"Hell, yes," Rich said. "Leah's where I finally got to second base with T."

"But not in reality?"

"Dude, there are three ways of getting into the Wodtke-Weirs' and I have tried two of them."

"Climb in through her window?"

Rich sniffed. "Better if you do these things by the book. You can get in the front door if you take a class with Dr. Weir. You can have dinner with him and his wife if you get straight sixes. Guess who was the last guy to pull a quintuple six."

"I don't know."

"Stephen Ha," he said.

"What's the third way of getting into her house?"

"You get in so much trouble that Weir has to kick you out."

"Get kicked out of Hale so, what, you can sit in Weir's library and wait for a chance to run up to Thomasina's room?"

"Right," Rich said. "I never knew how much I didn't know until I walked up to the Weirs' window one night and saw that their library has a second and third floor. There's no ceiling. The books just keep going up and up and up."

"To what?"

"To books by people whose last name starts with *A*," he said. "Thomasina told me it's the largest private library in Pennsylvania, but you can't read two-thirds of it because some guy put his foot through the rungs in the ladder to the second floor."

"Every rung?"

"Vaughn Warnicke. That guy in the engine room who's, like, six and a half feet tall." The "engine room" referred to the middle four seats in an eight-man scull in crew. Basketball had been my first love, but I had bad knees and no game and could only do sports where I could be sitting down, which meant crew or cycling, or Scrabble at schools where Scrabble is a sport. I had rowed at Clovis Friends and had never seen a rower in a library, so I liked the sound of this Vaughn Warnicke.

"So that's it — the ladder breaks and the books up there can never be read again?"

"Dr. Weir says he's waiting for the same kind of ladder to come up on eBay. I think he and my dad like it this way because the books at eye level are all by people like them whose names are near the end of the alphabet. The Rise of the Us and Revenge of the Ws."

"Like Urlacher?"

"Right," he said. "And like Wodtke, who's Weir's wife. And like Weir, who used to be a shrink and wrote about his patients."

"So what's up there? Dirty books? The Hale School's worst secrets?"

"Thomasina knows," he said. "Win, if she ever offers to meet you on the top floor of her father's library, well, that's not happening."

"Rich, if you need me to spend a night in the common room, then just say the word and I'll clear —"

Quickly — too quickly — Rich closed his eyes and turned his head away as if he wouldn't hear of putting me out of our room. "She and I aren't serious. Besides, you must be tired from your trip."

10

Rich and I lay awake in our beds on either side of the xylophone from hell — our clonking, clanking radiator — and talked late into the night. We couldn't figure out why the school had put us together. A lot of the kids at Hale had learning disabilities and others were just fuck-ups who'd been kicked out of other boarding schools. I was here because I did strange things like read the dictionary as if it were a book. Rich said he was here because he could barely read.

Rich told me about growing up in northeastern Ohio, on the banks of a river where rainbows swirled magically. Some rainbows were chemicals and could dissolve the soles off a cheap pair of shoes. Some rainbows were oil and caught fire on the Fourth of July, and Rich and his father would watch these fires floating in the dark. Thomas Urlacher was a writer of the old school who did not have email and kept the ringer on his phone off most of the time. Thomas had not been much of a father to Rich and his younger brother, and simply left his family after publishing his first book of poetry. He moved to Pennsylvania to be the writer-in-residence at a small college and did not answer Rich's letters asking when he would be back. Rich was ten and had been told that he read at a first grade level, and while he was terrified that his father found his letters embarrassing, Rich kept writing and would learn later that his father had included a few of these letters, misspellings and all, in his second book of poetry.

"That's sweet. I mean he must really love you to put you in his book."

"No," Rich said, "he put them in *as* poetry. I write and get Fs and get held back until I'm, like, the first kid in the history of the fifth grade who could grow a mustache. He picks my letters out of the trash and puts them in a book and people call it poetry."

"I'm sorry."

"So do you want to take his honors class with me?"

I laughed despite myself — a cackling sound that I could not control, as if Rich's father's cruelty had cast some kind of spell on me. "Yes," I said. "I mean — wait — he teaches here?" My dad had said that "girls all love his stuff," so a school for boys seemed like a strange choice for Thomas Urlacher.

"Orwell one-oh-one," Rich said. "It's for seniors but I might get in as his son."

"Is that his only class?" I said.

"He teaches composition, too, but for freaks and foreigners."

"Freaks?"

"Like Kenneth Duong, the California spelling king. Mostly Dad's been too busy writing since they made him the PA poet laureate."

"Ugh," I said, "does that mean he has to write about Pennsylvania?"

" 'Writing' is a strong word for what my father does."

This made zero sense to me. How could the poet laureate of Pennsylvania not be a writer? Sure there were ambassadors who only got their jobs after giving money to the president, and Britain had the House of Lords, but wasn't writing different? Mr. Urlacher sounded like a bastard to leave his kids and not write back to Rich. But if saying that his famous father was incapable of any writing — not just to him — helped Rich come to terms with him, then more power to Rich.

11

I liked Rich and was impressed by the degree to which he didn't let his father or Fitler or the Hale School get him down. He had lived in Fitler since his freshman year and had refused to move up to the third floor because a quirk of the pipes meant that sound traveled directly from some rooms on the third floor into Dr. and Mrs. Goltz's bedroom. Boys who lived up there sometimes got busted for *things they had not done yet*, while boys on the second floor could say anything so long as they whispered. Among Rich's skills was knowing the number of the one guy in Wyomingville, the closest town to Hale, who would deliver pizza at any time of day, and knowing the secret to passing the Hale swim test, a sadistic rite in which you were supposed to tread water for fifteen minutes with your wrists and ankles tied. "Sink," Rich said about the test, "the secret is to sink."

"So they'll pull you out?" I said.

"So you can push off the bottom and come up for air."

Rich could cook a three-course meal with nothing more than a heating coil, and when some older guys locked Rich in his room, he'd survived for three days by using the icicles outside his window to make soup and Kool-Aid and instant beef bourguignon.

"Why did they lock you in your room?"

Rich shrugged. "Because it was that or drink the black water burbling up from a hole in the basement."

"Why didn't you just climb down the fire escape?"

"Escape would have been seen as a sign of weakness."

12

The heat and the clanking of our radiator gave me nightmares, and I finally dragged my mattress across the room and lay breathing the cool air coming from the crack beneath our door. I heard a scratching sound through the floor, followed by Dr. Goltz cursing under his breath. He was chasing a mouse around his apartment . . . or just working on one of his rock specimens. I lay still for a long time and was facing the wall when I heard Rich climb out onto the fire escape.

"Rich?" I said.

He grabbed his pillow and lay down on the landing and said, "Go to sleep, dude."

I heard a chirping like some bird who was awake at night, but it was just Rich's phone letting him know that someone, somewhere, had just sent him a text. His phone chirped every few minutes for most of the rest of the night and I only fell asleep when the sky was turning gray and some crows began to caw excitedly.

I woke up to the blare of a neighbor's alarm clock — a horn and the first woman's voice that I'd heard at Hale, or almost a woman's voice. Speaking calmly through the blare was Mother, the computer from the movie *Alien* — "You have ten minutes to reach minimum safe distance . . . You now have nine minutes to reach minimum safe distance" — as if my neighbor's dream was about to turn deadly. Fitler had sagging ceilings and the rubbery floors of an insane asylum, and the walls were so thin that you could hear your neighbors breathe.

Rich was not in his bed and not on the landing. I got dressed and went downstairs and saw Dr. Goltz sitting in his office, hunched over his desk with his face pressed to a microscope. "Where were you last night?" he said.

He had not looked up and it took me a second to realize that Goltz was addressing me. He reached out and grabbed a mug and took a sip of coffee — all without looking up or moving his head so that he looked like a man pouring oil down a hatch.

"In my room. I'm sorry I never introduced myself."

"You need to sign in at night. Not signing in is the same as cruising, understood?"

"Yes, sir."

"Brownie?"

I hadn't seen the plate of brownies among the rocks on his desk. I grabbed one and it tasted bitter and stuck like sand to my tongue, and I must have made a face because Dr. Goltz laughed and said, "My wife makes them with beans instead of chocolate."

"Why?" I tried to say, but it came out, "Www?"

"Mrs. G has seen the way you boys eat at the Ratty. Believes you need more protein."

"The Ratty?"

"The Rathskeller Cafeteria."

"Sounded like you were chasing a rat around in here last night."

Goltz sat up. His red eyes and nose with its spray of burst capillaries made him look like a diver just back from the deep. "Trouble falling asleep?" he said.

"It was hot. Also freezing, damp. There's not even a word for it."

"I will see what I can do."

A pink crystal looked like cake. Sucking on a rock would have been preferable to Mrs. G's brownies. A toilet flushed and I felt a strange sense of kinship with Dr. Goltz — a man trying to concentrate with eighteen kids overhead, our bangs and groans amplified like noises on a ship. I looked around his office and saw photographs of Goltz digging in pits and photographs of ugly rocks that had been framed as if they were family. Goltz's Hale diploma hung above his desk and there seemed to be two things very wrong with it — a coffee stain that had blotted out the date and a big blank space where his name should have been. My father kept his master's in Soviet foreign policy on a shelf in his office — a man almost proud of his futility. I was about to ask Goltz about his blank diploma when my Jitterbug vibrated and Goltz — like most men of his generation — looked disgusted and personally offended that whoever was trying to call or text me didn't understand that I was already talking to him.

"Sorry," I said, and stepped into the hall.

dude u r too late

for what?

the preclass

i dont know what that is

the preclass where my dad decides wholl be in Orwell 101
is it over?
nding now

Rich had tried to get into his father's classes before and had never passed the pop quiz on the first day of class—usually on a book that Urlacher assumed all high school boys should have read. Orwell 101 was for seniors, and I thought I had no chance and nothing to lose by running like hell and showing up with sweat pouring down my face. The door was open and Rich's father wasn't there—just a quote on the blackboard in his pretty, cursive handwriting.

"Winston," Thomasina said.

There were two empty desks, one on each side of Thomasina Wodtke-Weir. Hose was right. She wore a gray skirt and drab gray stockings that made her look like a librarian or an English governess. The streak of gray in her brown hair was frightening, but Thomasina also had the most voluptuous lips and the haughty air of a teacher who has condescended to sit with her students.

"So what do we do?" I said, sitting next to her.

"Write five hundred words about *Nineteen Eighty-Four*."

"Where is Mr. Urlacher?"

"Getting us a new room," she said. "Too depressing for Tom—"

"Please don't call him 'Tom,'" Rich said.

"—to teach us Orwell in the basement."

"Does anybody have a copy of the book?" I said. All I really knew about *Nineteen Eighty-Four* was that the hero and I had the same first name and that he lived in a world in which they were trying to make language as simple as possible. Newspeak had no shades of gray and everything was "good," "ungood," "plusungood," or "doubleplusungood."

Several guys and Rich and even Thomasina laughed at me. They were still laughing when Mr. Urlacher walked in with a steaming cup of coffee in each hand and set one down on Thomasina's desk.

"Thanks, Tom," Thomasina said. "Win here was asking if there's a copy of the book?"

"This is a class for seniors who have read the book," he said, "or who know something about George Orwell. Kids, you have about another five minutes —"

"Ogre well ogre," I blurted out.

"Excuse me?"

"The letters in 'George Orwell' can be rearranged to spell —"

"Is this kid with you?" he said to Thomasina.

"No," she said.

I'd said a lot of dumb things in my life, but never this dumb, and felt my hands and feet go cold with horror. I stared at Thomasina's gray streak of hair and then stared into her purse. I saw pens and lipstick and a book I thought was *Nineteen Eighty-Four*. The quote on the board was the first sentence of the book, and I was trying to think of something, anything, to write when Mr. Urlacher clapped his hands and said, "Time."

He had not been impressed by my scrambling the letters in Orwell's name, so I went several steps further and rearranged the entire first sentence.

It was a bright cold day in April, and the clocks were striking thirteen.	*I was right. The bad ones teach. I drank coral pills. End tricky twittering.*

I signed my name and put my paper in the pile. Probably Thomas Urlacher would hate what I'd written and throw it in the trash. Although he'd thrown away his son's misspelled pleas to come home before giving some titles and calling them poetry.

I sat through U.S. history and precalculus, where each teacher gave the same speech about not committing plagiarism. Then I sat in the back row of Geology 101 and closed my eyes while Dr. Goltz gave this same speech and parts of other speeches I had heard through Fitler's pipes. The story about how kids in the old days were grateful to go to school on Saturdays instead of farming potatoes. The story about the coal mine owner who tied a string to the long hand on his clock so that the passage of a thirteen-hour shift took more like fourteen. The door opened and there seemed to be some row *behind* the last row of desks, as a girl sat behind me and exhaled heavily.

"There you are," Thomasina said. "I looked in the AP class but here you are in Rocks for Jocks."

Dr. Goltz had been writing something on the board and froze at the sound of Thomasina's voice. "Rocks for what?" he said to her.

"Your poem," she said, "they're reading it. I've seen them weigh papers and base the grade on the weight but they're actually reading yours."

"Is that good?"

"What for jocks?" said Dr. Goltz.

Thomasina ignored him and the twenty or so other guys in the room ignored her — guys whose shoulders were so big that they seemed to have no necks, other guys with the long, rubbery arms of swimmers or rowers. Thomasina grew up on campus and had been sitting in on classes since she was a little girl. I couldn't tell if guys were ignoring her the way they would a kitten or the way they would a bitchy old librarian.

Dr. Goltz came out from behind his desk and challenged her a third time. Thomasina seemed to think the rules did not apply to her—that Goltz and these boys and I were guests or neighbors to whom her father had forced her to say hello—but they still applied to me. "Granites for ingrates," I said.

"Granites for what?" said Dr. Goltz. "Ms. Wodtke-Weir, I don't see you on my list, and I'm going to have to ask—"

"See you later—"

"Are you joining us or just—"

"See you later, Win," she said.

13

I went to the library and got a copy of *Nineteen Eighty-Four* and read the first few chapters, confident I could talk my way into Orwell 101. I spent another long night sleeping on the floor, away from the xylophone from hell, and woke to find Rich climbing in through the window.

"Where've you been?"

"At breakfast."

"The Ratty doesn't open till six thirty."

"At a diner with my dad."

"Did I get into his class?"

Rich laughed. "I knew she would be your type."

Thomasina was my type and I didn't even try to defend myself. "So did I?"

"No, but my dad and Dr. Weir are deciding what to do about your poem."

Rich's phone chirped and I never had the chance to ask him what he meant. I grabbed my books and went downstairs and got by Dr. Goltz by cramming one of his wife's bean brownies into my mouth and by making a woofing noise when he asked me how I'd slept. I ran to the English building and walked right into the faculty lounge. I'd learned at Hannah Penn that you'll often find teachers smoking or drinking or looking at things online, and they won't dare kick you out. There was Thomas Urlacher, reading a copy of the *Derrick* with his feet up on a desk. The *Derrick* was the newspaper of the oil and gas industry in northeastern Pennsylvania and had been known to poach reporters and photographers from the *Hale Mountaineer*, offering them a small salary and something that was priceless — permission to be out after sign-in and work the late shift at the paper's office on Route 6.

Mr. Urlacher wore hiking boots that were both new and dirty, the soles looking like chocolate cake. He lived on a farm several miles west of Hale, somewhere in the hills, but he had the smooth, pale skin of a much younger man who rarely saw the sun. He was old around the eyes — with crow's feet and a red scar through one of his eyebrows — and old in the hands, where thick calluses scraped against the pages of his newspaper.

"Rich said you need to talk to me about my poem?" I said.

"Good morning to you, too," he said.

"Mr. Urlacher —"

"U," he said. "You can call me Mr. U."

"Did I get into your class? I love 'Love.' It's my favorite. And I read the book last night."

Mr. U lowered his newspaper and looked me in the eyes. He squinted even though I was right in front of him and I thought he might be one of those people who would rather not see than admit they need glasses. "Dr. Weir and I would like to talk to you about your poem."

"I can write about the book. I'm not a freak, not *just* a freak —"

"Winston, my son says you're smart and that you're nice to him —"

"I'm not," I said.

"Correction — not as mean as other boys about his disability. And he says you told him that your greatest ambition in life is to play a fifteen-letter word across three triple-word-score squares, thus bidecaseptupling your score. That is freakish. See you at six o'clock in Dr. Weir's library."

"Do you teach other classes?"

Mr. U groaned. "No," he said. "I mean they make me teach sophomore composition but you are a junior and it's not your cup of tea."

14

Mr. U looked worried, sick. What had I done that could be so terrible? This thought gnawed at me as I *hic*'ed and *hoc*'ed my way through Latin. I could not concentrate and talked about *Nineteen Eighty-Four* in U.S. history because I'd read it instead of doing my homework. And in a sign that I'd done something truly terrible — that I'd torn some hole in the Hale universe — my crew coach quoted my poem through his megaphone. I had just "caught a crab," pulling so hard that my oar flew over my head and hit the guy behind me. Coach Kashvilinski was telling us about the punishment for catching crabs in Russia when he seemed to realize just who had caught a crab. "Winston Crwth."

"Yes, sir," I said.

"'I was right. The bad ones teach.' What is meaning of this phrase?"

"Well, sir, there's a saying that people who can't do teach —"

"And people who can't teach teach gym," he said. "Now I am familiar."

The Skulking River runs along the base of the Endless Mountains, collecting rain and melting snow and sometimes salt and chemicals used to deice the roads, and on sunny days the water swirled with rainbows. I was a little more than six feet tall and Coach K had put me at starboard bow, behind the biggest guys in the boat's "engine room." The biggest, Vaughn Warnicke, rowed so hard that sparks flew off the wheels on his seat and I worried about these sparks landing in a rainbow and setting the water and our wooden scull on fire. But some days, when Jimmy Weems in bow was bashing me in the back and Coach K was making us row with our eyes closed, I *hoped* the boat would catch on fire and give us a reason to go home.

Bad teachers taught gym and bad or broken athletes seemed to end up on the crew team. Vaughn's first love was soccer, but he'd wrecked both knees and had them put back together with staples and titanium. Vaughn walked stiffly, and with his crew cut and the jagged scars on his legs, he looked a bit like Frankenstein. The stroke — the guy who sat in front of the coxswain and set the pace for the rest of us — had been the star pitcher on the baseball team until he got a concussion and could not remember how to throw his curveball. Jimmy Weems spent all of his spare time in Leah — the game that re-created the boarding school experience — where he was the star quarterback and wrote for Leah's newspaper.

Coach K was from Russia and had gone to Harvard on a crew scholarship. The Hale team practiced every day and Coach K's strategy was to compensate for our lack of strength, skill, and experience with sheer willpower. We rowed in the rain and Coach K promised that we would row in the snow. "You get day off once a year. For terrifying Hale swim test."

This was not a joke — Coach K was all muscle and sank like a stone after they tied his wrists and ankles together and asked him to tread water for fifteen minutes. Most guys on the team sank or gave up and lay gasping with their chins up on the side of the pool, looking like dying seals. After dismissing Rich as an idiot, I now believed absolutely in the Urlacher Way — that just because you couldn't read or swim didn't doom you to failure. Taking his advice, I sank to the bottom of the pool, then used the bottom to kick off and come up for air.

15

I ran to the Ratty and scraped the crust — the only part that any-body ate — off a steaming tray of turkey tetrazzini and added some potatoes and sat by myself at a long table like a boat. I put my phone on the table and took a long drink of lemonade and saw my phone crawling away through the bottom of my glass. I never got calls. My phone did not chirp or beep, but I must have set it on vibrate accidentally. Kids at Clovis Friends used to show each other calls from the hot area codes — 212 for New York, 323 for Los Angeles — but this was a 987 and probably a robocall.

My Jitterbug was dancing toward the edge of the table when I saw what seemed to be the second girl at the Hale School. She was Thomasina's height and wore rubber gloves, an apron, and a greasy gray hairnet that made her look like a crone. Behind her were several guys, some of whom I recognized, doing Ratty Duty, too. (Hale cut costs by having us clean the dorms and rake the leaves and wash the dishes ourselves.) This girl stood in the kitchen and was going through the messes that guys had left on their trays. Wobbling blobs of Jell-O caught the light and shim-mered as she threw them in the trash. Yellow lemonade in which grains of pepper swirled. Dirty napkins that some guy had balled up neurotically. A book so bloodied with ketchup that it seemed to be alive, and it was only when this girl began to read this book that I knew it was her and that Hale could not be such a bad place if even the headmaster's daughter got Ratty Duty.

"Eyes in the boat," Vaughn Warnicke said, and sat across from me.

"No, I want to see the girl."

"Also, you really shouldn't drink the lemonade."

"No?"

"It's got saltpeter. To keep guys from having sex."

"I don't need help with that."

"It's true. Rich gave some to Dr. Goltz."

"Goltz has sex?"

"Goltz has a kit that shows when something is poisonous. Kids have been bringing him stuff for years — the water from the Ratty and the water from Fitler and the water from the pool. The orange water from this old abandoned house in the woods."

"Does saltpeter work on girls?"

Vaughn shrugged. "I wouldn't know."

"You don't have a girlfriend?"

"Too much time in the boat and too much time in the tanks once the Skulking freezes."

Getting eight guys to row in sync in a tiny scull was a tricky business — made trickier by the Skulking's rocks and sharp turns and general unfitness as a place to row — and Coach K believed that looking left or right or even thinking *left* or *right* would cause a boat to wobble.

"The tanks?" I said.

"Sure," Vaughn said. "We need somewhere to row during Christmas break."

The crew team at Clovis Friends had done community service during the winter trimester — swimming with kids with cerebral palsy or muscular dystrophy — and I was horrified to learn that Vaughn and some other members of our team spent their winter break at Hale.

"Where do you live that you can't get home for winter break?" I said.

"With my mom. In California. Rich told me you're bicoastal,

too—that you grew up in Philly but also San Francisco." Vaughn stuttered slightly on "bicoastal" as if the word embarrassed him—almost as if he were talking about being bipolar and suffering from wild mood swings because he split his time between the East Coast and sunny California.

"Yes," I said, "my parents thought it would make me 'cosmopolitan.'"

"And did it?"

"My friends in Philly made fun of me for being a hippie and a word freak. My friends in California made fun of me for being a prig." In truth, I'd spent ten summers with my mother in California and had yet to make a friend. I played in Scrabble tournaments and played for money on the streets of Berkeley and was always making people mad by challenging Berkeley spellings like "womyn" or "herstory." I had two cousins in the Oakland Hills whom I babysat occasionally. And if little Giles and Juniper were the closest thing I had to friends in California, even they were freaked out when I refused to let Giles wear his sister's skirt to a play date, and when I insisted that "he" be used to refer to men and "she" to women.

"So a hippie prig?"

"I guess."

"So growing up on both coasts, in your case, made you embody the worst aspects of each coast?"

"You could say that, sure," I said.

"Look," Vaughn said, "I know I seem . . . I know you're smart and probably don't . . . What I'm trying to say is that you can talk to me. I'm not just a guy who grunts and can count to ten."

"No," I said, "I've heard you go as high as twenty-five."

"That's the spirit."

"What?" I said.

"The problem with Stephen Ha was that he never fought back. Stephen turned the other cheek, and he never knew how much we all loved him."

"Everyone loved Stephen Ha?"

Vaughn grinned. "That's very good," he said. "I can see you're different."

"You think I'm like Stephen Ha because I play Scrabble, too?"

Vaughn blushed. "Different" had to be good since Ha had killed himself, and I wanted to know more but it was almost six and I had to get to my meeting with Dr. Weir. I picked up Vaughn's tray and carried it and mine over to Thomasina and put them down in front of her. She picked up my dirty fork and threw it in a sink. "I've got one."

"One what?" I said.

"Diorites for idiots."

"What's a diorite?"

"A rock. I know you have your big meeting with my dad tonight. I was trying to cheer you up."

"Why won't your dad buy a new ladder for his library?"

"So boys can't climb up to my room?"

"There's the fire escape," I said. "Rich climbs down ours every night and doesn't come back till morning."

"Rich should be more careful."

"Where does he —"

"Shh," she said, and put a finger to her lips.

16

The Wodtke-Weirs lived on the bright side of the natatorium in an old stone house with high windows, a chandelier, and a rusty hitching post to which some people tied their dogs. A black dog named Loki was sitting by this post tonight, thumping his tail and simpering as if he was in trouble, too. Loki wore a leash and a studded collar, but he wasn't actually tied to the post, and I wondered why the poor thing didn't run away.

"Hello, Win," said Dr. Weir, opening the door for me. "Thanks for making time for us. I know how busy the first few weeks at Hale can be. Follow me. Usually, I like to do these things in my study but I thought we'd all be more comfortable in the library."

I did not like the sound of "all." I had the strange thought that I was in so much trouble that my mother had flown in from California. I was not far off as I saw Weir's wife, Dr. Gretje Wodtke, sitting in the library. Like her daughter, Dr. Wodtke had voluptuous lips and a gray streak of hair. Wodtke was the school's guidance counselor or one of its college counselors — I was not sure which — and it now occurred to me that I had been summoned to discuss not just my poem but my future.

"Hello, Win," Dr. Wodtke said. "Are you a coffee drinker?"

"Y—"

"I'm sorry?"

"Yes," I said. My mother did this all the time — interrupt me before I could speak — and it used to drive me wild. She was hard of hearing and would interrupt to be polite, if such a thing is possible, assuming I had spoken and that it was her turn again. Dr. Wodtke's eyes were bright and gray, suggesting a fierce, impatient intelligence.

"Hello, Win," Mr. U said with a sigh, sounding as if he, too, was in trouble. He sat in the corner and did not look up at me. "Glad that you could come and talk."

"So you're a coffee drinker?" Dr. Wodtke said again, her lips pursed and her eyebrows arched as if "yes" was still not good enough, or as if she wanted to give me a chance to say more about this relatively safe subject before we moved on to Orwell, poetry, and my attack on the teaching profession.

"Well," I said, "I used to look at the coffee drinkers at my old school and think they were the smart kids —"

"And which of your old schools was that?" she said.

"Hale," I almost said. Wodtke's harsh voice hurt my ears and the shadows on her wrinkled face made her look a bit like Miss Havisham in *Great Expectations* — a woman who was left at the altar and lived forever after with her petrified wedding cake. I don't mind being wrong but can fall to pieces when people prove me wrong. "Hannah Penn High," I said.

"She was great," Mr. U said.

"Yes —" I said, but stopped myself before Wodtke could cut me off.

Mr. U saw I was drowning and now threw me a line. "Penn's memoirs are supposed to be amazing. I can almost reach the Ps when I stand on a chair."

I looked up to where I thought the Ps would be and felt as if I would fall up and out of my chair and crash into the ceiling. The walls sloped together as they rose, and then *seemed* to slope together because they were so far away, and the whole effect was like sitting in a ziggurat. Rich had said his father and Dr. Weir were happy when the ladder broke and people were forced to read just books by Urlacher and Weir and other writers near the end of the alphabet. But I noticed something else about the top two floors of the library — in several places the books had been removed entirely and replaced with busts, portraits, a wooden box, a gray rock and a lump of coal, a chess set in which the figurines were all people and in which the kings were stooped over tiny games of chess, a basketball that was covered with signatures, and a Hale diploma. Tapping a finger on his leg, Mr. U also seemed to be pointing at this chess set and suggesting that I take a closer look.

Stiffening, Dr. Wodtke said, "But, Winston, you changed your mind about the smart kids —"

"When one of them threatened me physically." I wanted to tell her about the boy at Hannah Penn who threatened to cut my tongue out for saying "cwm" to his girlfriend — a story that never failed to win people's sympathy — but something about Mr. U tapping, typing on his leg made me think that he was *transcribing* this meeting and that I would become the tragic, tongueless hero of some epic poem called "Cwm."

"I'm sorry," Dr. Wodtke said. "That sounds truly horrible."

"My dad drinks the stuff and I've been drinking it since an early age, and if you want to know the truth, I can never get enough."

"Neither can Thomasina. You know she wouldn't touch 'the stuff' for the longest time. The boys who drink it as freshmen are the ones smoking and pretending to bake cakes by the time they're seniors." I had seen Rich and a couple of other guys "bake a cake" — suck the nitrous oxide from the little torpedoes used to make whipped cream for cakes — but kept a blank look on my face for Dr. Wodtke's sake. "But then she met your roommate, Rich, and I don't know what he did but she drinks so much that her skin is turning brown."

I laughed. Dr. Wodtke narrowed her gray eyes and seemed to think that talking about coffee — her idea in the first place — had been some kind of trap and compromised her authority. "Andrew?" she said to her husband.

"Yes. Right. So, Winston, we have several questions about your poem and why you chose —"

"The kid had never read a word of Orwell and came up with that in less than five minutes," Mr. U blurted out. I grinned like an idiot and hid it with my coffee cup. The poet laureate of Pennsylvania liked my writing and was standing up for me! "Less time than it took William Carlos Williams to write 'This Is Just to Say' and apologize for eating all the plums in the icebox."

"Winston's intelligence is not the issue here," Dr. Weir said. "Young man, what we want to know is why you drank coral pills."

"Pills?" I said.

"In your poem you said, 'I drank coral pills.'"

Mr. U clapped his hands. "See?" he said. "It's like *Rain Man*. The kid can do it but can't remember doing it."

"I know what I wrote," I said. Mr. U seemed to think that I had Asperger's or autism, but people thought that all the time. And as Mr. U grinned I saw that he was a kid at heart and that, for Rich, being a kid's kid must have been miserable. "I'm not going to kill myself, if that's what you're wondering."

Dr. Weir began to speak but his wife interrupted him. "Were they coral-colored pills," she said, "or the coral pills they write about on the Internet?"

"I did not eat pills," I said.

"Are you on Twitter?"

"No," I said.

"Did you send your note out to the rest of the school? Is that why you wrote 'End tricky twittering?'"

"It was not a note," I said.

"Then why was it addressed to Thomasina?"

"What?" I said.

"There are six *T*s in the first sentence of *Nineteen Eighty-Four* — I checked — and seven *T*s in what you wrote."

"That was a mistake," I said.

"Winston, you understand that we're only trying to help?"

"No," I said, "I think you dropped the ball and failed to see the signs that Stephen Ha was going to kill himself. Like writing a suicide note in front of several hundred people. Now you see signs everywhere that kids are going to kill themselves."

"Why did you sink and sit at the bottom of the pool?"

"You're kidding."

"Don't yell," she said.

"The whole point of the test is that they tie your arms and legs together so that you can barely move," I said.

"Darling," said Dr. Weir, "I don't know if that's fair. Winston is a little thin . . ."

Mr. U looked me in the eyes — the sad, handsome, pleading eyes of an old Labrador. I didn't really hear the rest of Dr. Weir's speech . . . something about boys, girls, body fat, and different kinds of intelligence. Mr. U looked at a book or something overhead and I guessed it was the chess set or the Hale diploma.

"Winston," Dr. Weir was saying, "I showed your poem to Dr. Goltz and he let us know about a similar incident."

"Similar to rearranging the letters in the first sentence of *Nineteen Eighty-Four*?" I said.

"He says you're sleeping on the floor, which is fine, a lot of boys find it more comfortable. But Goltz says you couldn't say if your room was hot or cold. Or rather it was both, or 'there was no word' for it, or that you seemed to be suffering from aphasia. Do you know what aphasia —"

"It's the inability to put thoughts into words," I said. "Hey, is the king in that chess set supposed to be Bobby Fischer?"

Mr. U shook his head and I saw I'd chosen wrong. But before I could ask about the diploma, Dr. Weir had grabbed the kings and handed them to me. "A gift from a friend who played against Fischer once. The white king is supposed to be Fischer as a boy. The lips, the Beatle haircut, and the penetrating gaze. The black king is supposed to be Fischer when he was old."

"Old and insane," Mr. U said. "Fischer lived alone and played chess against himself and developed wild ideas about Hitler and the Jews. That black king is supposed to look like a complete lunatic."

"I don't know," I said. "He looks more like Solzhenitsyn."

Dr. Weir grinned at this and even his wife seemed to frown with pleasure — frown as if suppressing a smile of relief. "Well," she said, "we have a student of Russian history."

"The son of a student who spent six years trying to get his Ph.D. in SoFoPo," I said, "only to have the Soviet Union suddenly go belly-up."

Mr. U said, "Solzhenitsyn dug a tunnel from his house to the barn where he wrote, as if stepping outside would wreck his concentration. He got his wife to do absolutely everything — some people say his interviews and some say his writing."

"Winston," Dr. Wodtke said, "are you telling us that this black king looks like Solzhenitsyn? Or that Solzhenitsyn looks like a lunatic?"

"I think Solzhenitsyn spent several decades writing a definitive history of the Soviet Union — a place that no longer exists. Dr. Weir, I'm curious, why is your diploma blank?"

A wild and brilliant guess that crushed Weir in his seat — his shoulders sank and his chin fell and his hairy hands sagged into his crotch. "All schools have their traditions," Weir said feebly.

"Dr. Goltz's was blank, too. Did you guys graduate?"

"Not on graduation day. Hale has a rule that you can't fail any of your final final exams, or fail a class your last semester, or fail to pay your activity fee for your senior year, or, in my case, fail to return your books on time to the library. That's why my diploma's blank. At the time I swore I would never set foot on the grounds of the Hale School again. Now, of course, I'm the headmaster."

"And Goltz?"

"I'll let Dr. Goltz tell you his story. Winston, I'm pleased and impressed by the way you've handled yourself in this interview and I want to offer you every opportunity to make the most of your abilities."

"My abilities?" I said.

"Let's be frank. Surviving Hale depends on finding something, anything, to give yourself a sense of purpose and make your fellow students treat you with respect. For some boys it's academics and for some boys it's sports. Take Rich. He has a terrible time with his schoolwork and doesn't care for sports but is very happy here because he is so popular." Rich was happy because he was going out with the only girl at Hale — perhaps the only girl who would ever go to Hale.

I held my tongue while Dr. Weir talked about my "abilities." Weir said I was good with words and "thinking outside the box." "Winston, you may be good with words but you need to understand that words have *meanings*. Mr. Urlacher has agreed to work with you and let you into his class —"

"His Orwell?" I interrupted him.

"No, his composition."

A class for kids from China and Central America and other kids for whom English was not their first language. Also kids like Rich with severe dyslexia.

"But can't I take Orwell, too?"

"No," Mr. U said, "that wouldn't be fair to Rich and all the other kids whose writing wasn't good enough. But I'd like to work with you."

"I can write —"

"It's not writing if —"

"If, what, I didn't copy it straight from the dictionary?"

"Winston, what I'm trying to say is that I'll be your Scrabble coach."

Part Two

17

So began my happiest time at the Hale School for Boys, a time when my faults were forgiven and I felt hopeful, safe, and strangely popular. Dr. Weir shook my hand warmly at the end of our interview and gave me a swollen paperback from his library. It looked like a history of the Johnstown Flood but turned out to be a book of poems by Mr. Urlacher. Then I walked home to find the common room lit up by candles and Mrs. Goltz serving brownies made with chocolate. I knew this had to be a coincidence — that Dr. Weir had not put the whole school on a Winston Crwth suicide watch — but I felt as if she had added chocolate for my sake, and the smiles on all our faces were so wide, so naked, that Mrs. Goltz blushed in embarrassment.

I slept well that night and came home from my morning classes to find an air conditioner in our room. Dr. Weir had taken my description of the temperature in Fitler — "there's no word for it" — as a cry for help or another possible sign of mental illness. Humiliation that I no longer minded if it meant cool air and deep, untroubled sleep.

Nor did I mind sitting with the foreign kids and the Americans in Composition 101 and learning English as if it were my second language. I had always known there was something deeply wrong with me — what kind of kid hears "O evil you" when his mother says "I love you"? — and I was grateful for the chance to learn to use English like a normal high school kid. Something about this class focused Mr. U, too, so that he cocked his head and swung a hand back and forth as if conducting an orchestra. He made us write papers without using "good," "bad," "very," "like," or any form of "to be," and it was the native speakers who found this impossible — "is" slipped out no matter how hard we tried to stop it — and many of us failed these assignments.

The other boys in Fitler began dropping by our room and asking if I wanted to play cards or study or "do crossword puzzles" — their idea of what I did alone in my room at night. At first I thought that Dr. Weir or Dr. Goltz had sent these kids to be my friends out of pity or as some kind of punishment, but their rooms were hellishly hot, too, and they were hanging out with me because of the air conditioner. One or two played Scrabble and whispered obscenely when I played Q words without a U, or did things like put an X on the end of CHATEAU.

But for all of my sudden popularity, and Dr. Weir's decision to have a Scrabble club again, we could not get enough kids to make the club official. Hale abolished the Scrabble club after Stephen Ha killed himself. The fact that he wrote his note in a Scrabble game in front of several hundred people had led several schools in Pennsylvania to ban the game entirely. For Hale, this put Scrabble on a blacklist with Dungeons & Dragons — banned in the '80s because people thought it was Satanic — and Naked Twister — banned after the one time a girl played and put her right hand on blue and her left leg on red. And it joined a long list of things like cough syrup, Sudafed, Stilton, nutmeg, and mulberries, which were all "yellow flags" for drug use and other problems because these things, in large quantities, were hallucinogens.

I learned all of this by reading old copies of the school newspaper and by talking to Rich when he climbed back in through the window each morning — the only time I really saw him now that I was spending my evenings at Scrabble club, or studying in the library so I'd get good grades and not get kicked out of Scrabble club. Rich had been a freshman when Ha was a senior and was so embarrassed when they played the normal way, by keeping score, that Ha took pity and offered to play a game by "winter rules."

"So what are winter rules?" I said.

Rich mumbled something unintelligible. His mouth was full of pins he'd pulled from the arms and neck of one of his pink Oxford shirts — shirts he wore when he'd had an especially rough night and needed a fresh glaze under the day-old doughnut of his face.

"I'll show you. Play a word," he said.

I stuck my hand into the bag and had drawn seven tiles when it occurred to me that winter rules, whatever they were, may have been responsible for Stephen Ha's suicide. Like him, I was a Dark Scholar and a hopeless Scrabbler, and I had the sudden urge to put my tiles back ... except I could feel two Ss and was pretty sure that I could play a seven-letter word.

" 'Priests,' " I said.

"Too difficult."

" 'Sprites.' "

"No proper nouns," Rich said authoritatively.

"But a sprite is like a girl," I said.

"Oh, duh — right. But would you mind playing 'stripes'?"

I switched the P with the T. Rich gave me a tie with stripes.

"That's it?" I said. "That's idiotic."

"It's better when you play with girls."

"You bring Thomasina things?"

"And sometimes we do the verbs. What's another word for 'sex'?"

"You're kidding."

"No," he said.

"To make her have sex with you? Why not just play 'sex'?" I said.

"I did," he said, "now Thomasina thinks that every word I play is another guess for sex."

"So 'sex' didn't work?" I said.

"No," Rich said, "I'm thinking she has some other word for it, like the Eskimos have thirty-two words for 'snow,' or that you need to play the word off something else."

"Like?" I said.

"Like 'love' where the *e* is the *e* in 'sex,'" he said. The idea that Thomasina would fall in love with Rich because he played LOVE was, if anything, even more ridiculous than having sex for SEX, but Rich had cocked his head and had a thoughtful, almost scholarly, expression on his face.

The more I got to know this kid who could barely read and the more I got to know his dad, the more these two Urlachers seemed to have in common. His father was happiest when teaching kids for whom English was their second language, or when he found a poem in a restroom or the dictionary and didn't have to wrestle with writing it himself. Rich, conversely, claimed to hate school and books but was a philosopher king when it came to breaking and bending the rules at Hale. Rich was the first kid in the history of the school to arrange his schedule so that his first class started at 10 A.M. And for reasons that I did not understand, Rich seemed to have permission to be outside at night.

"I bought a thesaurus but those words are hard to play."

"Which words are hard to play?"

"'Copulate.' Also 'fornicate.' Also, I tried dirty words but they only made things worse."

18

The first meeting of Scrabble club was in the Fitler common room, a dank place with an old black-and-white TV that whined even when you turned it off and a soda machine that buzzed and would not give you Mountain Dew, the soda with the most caffeine, but gave out apple juice for free if you knew where to kick. The only kids to show up for the first meeting were Hose and I. Mr. U frowned and kept looking at his watch.

"What's wrong?" I said.

"We need three people to make it a club."

"We have three."

"Adults don't count. Where is she? Did one of you do something to scare Thomasina off?"

"I google her," said Hose.

"Actively?"

"Ongoingly."

Mr. U's jaw dropped a bit as if to make another *a*—as if he wanted to say, "And?" Then his pink tongue appeared and tapped to make a *d* instead: "Does she know you google her?"

"No."

"Then that doesn't count," he said.

"I could go get Rich," I said.

"My son plays by winter rules," Mr. U said dismissively.

"So," I said, "what's the problem if there are just two of us?"

"It means that we're not a club," he said. "And if we're not a club then I don't get credit for coaching a club."

Hale students might have it rough, with Hale's rules, lousy food, and classes on Saturdays. But I'd come to realize that our teachers had it worse. Dr. Goltz was in the middle of a twenty-year sentence as Fitler's housemaster, after which he and his wife would be given a stone house of their own. Coach Kashvilinski looked lonely and shrank an inch or two when he wasn't yelling at us through his megaphone, and would spend his evenings reading the library's three copies of *Izvestia*, all from 1968.

"Wait," I said, "you're the poet laureate and you have to coach a sport? Hale is that desperate?"

"No," he said, "Pennsylvania is that desperate. It's a miracle that this state has a poet laureate. The deal — I'm told the deal — was that I have to be a person, too."

"What?"

"I don't hunt, or drive a truck, or go to football games, or do much else to promote Pennsylvania. Linda doesn't do any of those things, either, but I guess that's why she needs a manly poet laureate."

"Linda?" I said.

"I'll never be Sir Walter Raleigh."

"Who's Linda?"

"Queen Elizabeth sent him to find El Dorado, which of course did not exist, but he got rich anyway by writing about his failure."

"Okay, but what do you mean —"

"I helped her find El Dorado and I'm even writing about El Dorado, but it's like she wants me to drill the wells myself."

"Helped?" I said.

"Linda King LaRue, the governor of Pennsylvania. LaRue loved 'Love' and appointed me, but she hasn't liked much since."

I did not follow politics — a field in which the words were, for the most part, too long or too new to be usable in Scrabble — but now dimly remembered reading about Dark Oil & Gas flying LaRue to Florida to see the Steelers in the Super Bowl.

" 'Dark Money Fuels LaRue's Machine,' " I said.

"Nice," he said.

"No, I read that in the *Inky*, the *Inquirer*. Does Dark mean Dark Oil and Gas?"

"Dark means Dark Oil and Gas, and it means they gave their money through a Super PAC to make it untraceable, and it's a reference to LaRue allowing fracking in state parks — except in the Dark Park where her mother and father live."

"The what?"

"Cherry Springs State Park," he said, "which is the second-darkest spot in the eastern United States. Linda lived there as a kid and loves to talk about how she hates pollution, but what people fail to understand is that Linda's talking about *light* pollution."

"How did a girl from the middle of nowhere get to be the governor?"

"She didn't. Linda was the lieutenant governor when the governor died. But to answer your question, a woman could be elected governor by being terrible on women's rights. Do you know the saying 'Only Nixon could go to China'?"

"No."

"Only a Neanderthal — a female Neanderthal — could be elected governor of Pennsylvania."

"So why you?"

"Do you think milk is the best drink in Pennsylvania? The Great Dane our finest dog? Or do you think some state senator owned some cows, and another lost everything but his Great Dane in his divorce? Why would the position of poet laureate be any different?"

"Is this about fracking?"

"Yes. Ever been to Harrisburg?"

"Once," I said. "My grandfather was going to surprise his girl-friend, a state senator, and sent me to bring her down to the café in the basement, but I couldn't find her office because the rooms that start with six are all on the fifth floor, and the rooms that start with five are all on the second."

"Ha!" he said, and slapped his knee. "That's Harrisburg for you! Do you know the one about how politics is show business for the ugly?"

"No."

"State politics is show business for ugly people who can't remember their lines."

Making a living as a poet seemed extremely difficult — worse than Scrabble since poets can't hustle people on the street. I used to think that Mr. U had it made. I was wrong. He said the job came with all the pressures of being an elected official but few of the perks, and that he never had time for his own work because he had to write poems for special occasions like the first day of spring, or the opening of a bridge, or the fracking of the first well in the Northern Tier.

19

All fall I played Scrabble with Hose and Mr. U, waiting for a third member to join our club and make it official. Or I played against JANE, an old computer on the third floor of the library — a relic from the late '80s that knew lots of '80s slang but, pathetically, did not have the ability to challenge words, so that I would sit down to find exchanges like this on her screen.

JANE: It's your turn, Rich.
RICH: URXQZIT

I'd heard Rich say this to Thomasina — "You are exquisite" — and saw her roll her eyes. Either way my roommate was intimate with the only girl and the closest thing to a second girl — a computer with a girl's name — at the Hale School for Boys. "Just unplug her and put her in the common room" was Hose's suggestion. "Tell Mr. U that Jane is a real girl and that JANE is her computer."

A casual observer of the Hale School for Boys — like my mother, who subscribed to the *Hale Mountaineer* — could get the impression that there were three girls at Hale. "So this Thomasina is dating your roommate," my mother said. "Jane plays Scrabble. You and she —"

"JANE is a computer. I need a third person to be in our Scrabble club."

"Or that boy Jimmy Weems who writes for the newspaper and spends all of his time with Leah —"

"Leah is a game," I said. "It's like Myst. That game you liked because the plants were so life —"

"Then how about Linda King LaRue? Or, no, wait — you're going to tell me that LaRue is just an app or the real governor's identity on Twitter."

This was Mom, the WiFi freak who worked all day in the dirt. "LaRue's out of my league," I said, giving up and going with the idea that Thomasina, JANE, Leah, and LaRue were all potential girlfriends. "Mr. U said she's a lawyer and used to be a lobbyist. She was Miss Northern Tier and used the money for law school."

"So she's from New York?" she said. "I thought New York banned fracking —"

"No, Mom, the Northern Tier is in the northern part of Pennsylvania, south of the Southern Tier in New York —"

"So why not get LaRue to be in your Scrabble club?"

"I don't think —"

"I'm serious. I heard there's this tournament where the winner gets five hundred bucks and a chance to play a game with her. Apparently, your lawyerly beauty queen of a governor is also a Scrabbler." Mom had done some strange things to play in Scrabble tournaments — cutting her hair and shaving her upper lip so she could join a league of hedge fund guys in San Francisco, or wearing sunglasses and keeping her eyes closed so she could play in a tournament for blind people — so the fact that she knew about this chance to play LaRue did not seem suspicious.

"Sure," I said, "except I need a third person now. Otherwise no club, no trip, no meeting with the governor."

"So Thomasina —"

"Is amazing but I think she's mad at me. She plays Rich, who can barely read, but she won't play with me."

"What about in Leah?"

"What?"

"Is she mad at you in there, too?"

"I don't play. It's no better than being at the real Hale. You still have to take classes and you need permission to have a girl in your room."

"Is there Scrabble?"

She was right. Jimmy Weems played football in Leah, and Leah's newspaper, with its ads and editorials about life in Leah, was more popular than Hale's real newspaper, and it seemed very likely that Leah would have Scrabble, too.

I created Windom Crude — the way my name had sounded through Stacy Yant's retainer — and wandered around Leah's Hale-like campus, looking for Thomasina or, at least, a Scrabble set. The flowers and the trees and some of the kids lying on the grass looked sick, until I realized that I was walking on the dark side of the natatorium and that *things really looked like this.* I walked around to the bright side and now the trees and kids looked fake — hard to have it both ways, I guess. Inside Dreissegacker was a Coke machine and a TV playing what looked like actual ads, one for Dark Oil & Gas, another for Alivert, an acne medication. Leah was a lot like Hale in that you had to take classes and be in your dorm by sign-in, and I thought I might as well take the Leah swim test. The idea was the same — swimming for fifteen minutes with your wrists and ankles tied — but I got distracted by the sight of a girl in the pool and this is how Windom drowned.

I died several more times — the game was maddeningly difficult, and food and other basic necessities were scarce — and finally learned that the school's only Scrabble set was in the headmaster's house. You could only enter by getting straight sixes or getting into so much trouble that he had to expel you. Straight sixes was doable — you didn't have to actually write all the papers the way you did in reality — and I studied harder than I ever had at Hale, taking advanced chemistry and writing down mnemonics like "OIL RIG" to help me remember that, when adding or subtracting electrons, Oxidation Is Loss, but Reduction Is Gain. I wrote in my book, a thing I never did in life, but then also lost the book, which I almost never do. I had a chemistry test in less than an hour of game time and, of course, could have logged off and studied in reality, but that seemed like cheating.

I saw my chemistry teacher eating a salad and asked if I could borrow his book. This is how I found the flaw in Leah's universe. "OIL RIG" and all of my other notes were in his copy of the book.

"Who wrote these?" I typed at him.

"I don't know," he said. "I think it's some kind of glitch."

"Are you real?"

"Are you?" he said. "What kind of name is Windom Crude? Sometimes I think that half the people in here work for Dark Industries."

The glitch extended to Scrabble, and I saved myself the trouble of taking the test or getting straight sixes by walking to Scranton — a trip that would take more than a day in reality — and buying a Scrabble set. Leah seemed infinite but the trick — the glitch — was that some things appeared in several places at once. That was the only way to explain why the score sheets in the set I bought in the Steamtown Mall had in fact been filled up with games between T, who I took to be Thomasina, and her opponent, D. She was playing after all, and must not have joined our club because of Mr. U or me. Here she played brilliantly but it was D who got the highest score I'd ever seen: 818. A number that had to be a lie. My high score was 591 and the all-time high was 770 by some kid in Massachusetts.

20

I read all of Mr. U's poetry and reread it for clues about how to write for Composition 101. "Write a poem without using any nouns or verbs." "Find a poem in this building and bring it to me by the end of class today." Many of his own poems had been found in restaurants or in the trash, or only after diving deep, deep into piles of old newspapers. Or he wrote poems named for towns in Pennsylvania. "Oil City" is about a girl who falls in love with a roughneck and follows him from her hometown of Oil City, Pennsylvania, all the way to Oklahoma. Another poem was about a woman living in the shadow of Three Mile Island. "Intercourse" sounded promising but it, too, was the name of a town in Pennsylvania. "Dark Park" rhymed and this made me think it was some kind of Scrabble poem.

"Did you call my mother?"

"What?" Mr. U slumped in his chair, his coffee cup tipping and the drops of coffee spattering his boots like mud. He had developed a deep, rattling cough and had grown more and more exhausted since the beginning of the semester, and sometimes forgot himself and gave us the same assignment two or three days in a row.

"Did you call—"

"Look, Win," he said. "I don't even have email. But I called and asked permission to take you to Harrisburg. I liked the sound of your mother in your application—'a gardener in Oakland, California'—but I have to say that I've never had a woman sound so disinterested—"

"Dirt in her iPhone and she's hard of hearing."

"Oh," he said.

"Makes my father wonder, too."

Mr. U claimed he couldn't get a meeting with LaRue, but I also wondered if he was ashamed to meet with her. Like *Nineteen Eighty-Four*'s Winston Smith, he seemed to shave with a blunt razor and the nicks on his face took a long time to heal. He yawned uncontrollably while listening to us read, and I saw he had canker sores in his mouth. Everyone agreed that our teacher looked like hell, and my first thought was that he was writing something big and that this thing was killing him. Many of the books we read for Composition 101 were by authors who killed themselves, or who tried to kill themselves, or who seemed to live lives of profound loneliness. Flannery O'Connor had lupus and lived with her mother and kept peacocks for company. Carson McCullers's husband divorced her, then remarried her, then committed suicide. Trevonia Dark's only son was severely handicapped and her husband was an alcoholic. Other brilliant writers had trouble with their eyes—Herman Melville as a result of scarlet fever, while James Joyce had glaucoma—but Mr. U saw fine and looked more like a man wracked by nightmares or insomnia.

I wanted to ask why Trevonia Dark was on this list but did not have the nerve. She and Ian, the CEO of Dark Oil & Gas, were divorced but still gave their scholarships together.

"Mr. U?" said Kenneth Duong, a boy from Little Saigon in San Jose, California. "I get why we're reading Joyce. And I guess I see how there's a fine line between genius and insanity. But, I mean, Trevonia Dark? Her poems are cookie recipes."

"Do you mean *like* cookie recipes?"

"No," he said, "I mean they actually —"

"Kenneth," Mr. U announced, "the woman of whom you speak may be our next poet laureate."

A teacher at Clovis Friends had been suspended after it came out that his wife had left him shortly before he made his students spend a semester reading books about men driven to murder, madness, or suicide by their wives leaving them. So I read ahead and saw that Mr. U had assigned several books by men and women who may have been his rivals. I mentioned this to my father — who, pathetically, still got calls from his old colleagues in the defunct field of SoFoPo, asking him to buy their books and promote their theories about the rise and fall of Communism on Facebook — and he used two Cold War sayings to explain Mr. U's behavior: "Know thine enemy" and "Keep your friends close but your enemies closer."

"Poets have archenemies?"

"If they're any good," my father said. "Son, I'd love to see you win this tournament in Harrisburg, or get out of your room, but I have to say it sounds like Mr. U is just using you to get a meeting with LaRue."

"I don't care."

"Why not?" he said.

"Because I want to meet her, too."

21

Kenneth Duong was my rival in Composition 101 and I applied my father's Cold War philosophy to him. Kenneth was the spelling king of California and had come in third at the National Spelling Bee in Washington, D.C. Like me, Kenneth knew a lot of words but couldn't put them together to the Hale School's satisfaction, and it was a black mark against spelling and Scrabble that its two champions were in Composition 101.

I watched this spelling bee on ESPN every year, wishing it was Scrabble, and I remembered Kenneth well. Most kids looked brittle, frozen, and miserable, and shuffled on- and offstage with the slow, defeated steps of circus animals. Kenneth was the fattest Asian kid I'd ever seen but he wore it happily. He had braces, which forced him to speak extra carefully, so that he popped his *P*s and buzzed his *J*s and *Z*s in a way that seemed to hurt the judges' ears. For the finals Kenneth wore a suit and tie and gold cuff links and looked like he was going to break out in song. Unlike the other kids, and unlike the people I saw at Scrabble tournaments, Kenneth had the swagger of a boxer unbroken by his bout with English. I longed to know his secret.

My chance came when Kenneth and I got Ratty Duty together and I did something dumb. Kenneth had fast hands and liked to work the conveyer belt where guys put their dirty trays — trays on which he would find pens, pencils, cell phones, books, and the occasional pink clam of a retainer. My job was to mop up messes in the dining hall and restock the milk machine — hoisting the huge plastic udder of milk over my shoulder and trying to cram the teat through a small opening. After several days I got good enough at these things that Kenneth gave me the very fun job of dunking racks of dirty glasses into a kind of steam bath. At least once a meal the dining hall would break into applause after some guy dropped a glass and it shattered audibly. I was carrying one of these racks back to the milk machine when I tripped and tilted the entire rack of thirty-six glasses in such a way that a single glass flew into the air. Instinctively, I lunged and made what I thought was a great catch ... except I dropped the rack and broke the other thirty-five, a clonking, crashing sound like I had thrown a xylophone through a window. Among those standing to applaud were Rich, Thomasina, Vaughn, and the entire football team.

"A real potato moment," Kenneth Duong said to me.

"A what?" I said.

"A moment when people see how dumb you are."

"Is that a Hale thing?"

"I don't know. Someone said it to me once and I've been waiting for the right moment to say it."

"To me?"

"To anyone."

"But you don't know what it means."

Kenneth shrugged. "Since when do Scrabble players care about meaning?"

This was true. People memorized lists of *Q* words without *U*s and seven- and eight-letter words, often without bothering to learn what they meant. Playing Scrabble, you forget what all words mean, and this is how Stephen Ha could say he was going to off himself in front of an audience.

Kenneth got down on his knees and stuck a dustpan into the pile of broken glass with a sound like shoveling salt. The mess was my fault but all I could do was stand there and let him sweep the broken glass off my shoes . . . and all I could think about was how much harder it would be to learn every word in the dictionary *and* their meanings. "Kenneth, do you mind if I ask you a question about s-p-e-l-l-i-n-g?"

"No," he said.

"What's your secret?"

"How did I become the best speller in California?"

"How did you get so good without it making you miserable?"

"Easy," Kenneth said. "The age limit for competitive spelling is fourteen and I always knew that I'd be retired soon."

22

Rich kept sneaking out at night and I learned his secret — or part of his secret — when he closed his eyes and began to breathe deeply while sitting at his desk. Blue gunk like ink or clay was jammed beneath his fingernails. The blue gunk smelled like ink and clove cigarettes, although Rich's hands usually smelled like cloves. Remembering the girl who asked if I wanted to "pull a Penn" on her, and remembering what Rich said about "doing the verbs," I wondered if Rich and Thomasina were writing on each other.

"Dude," Rich said, "why are you trying to smell my fingers?"

"Is this ink?"

"It is," he said.

"Since when —"

"I'm a reporter for the *Mountaineer* now."

"That's great!" I punched his arm and Rich punched me back appreciatively. "But isn't it just online now?"

"No, we're doing something with the *Derrick* and they still use ink, okay?"

Late that night I heard a bonging sound and I knew that Rich was climbing down our fire escape, or that someone was climbing up to our room. The Hale School had a lot of rules involving feet. A boy was not allowed to have a girl in his room unless he kept the door open and he and the girl kept at least three feet on the floor. A boy was not allowed to set foot outside his dorm between the hours of 10 P.M. and 6 A.M., 11 P.M. for seniors, although he was free to sit on the landing of a fire escape or dangle from the ladder so long as his feet did not actually touch the ground. Sneaking outside at night was known as "cruising." At Hannah Penn "cruising" meant riding with the windows down and the music cranked way up in some older kid's car. The kid might not have a license and might have been drinking, but it was widely believed that these things were not a problem if you were just a passenger.

I looked out the window, hoping to see the brown hair and voluptuous lips of Thomasina Wodtke-Weir. I saw Rich standing with both feet on the ground. Hale had its "two strikes and you're out" rule for cruising and for other major infractions. But in the same way that I used to believe some of the foolish graffiti in my bio book at Hannah Penn — "a girl can't get pregnant the first time that she has sex" — I thought I would not get caught my first time outside at night.

I climbed down the fire escape and followed Rich into the woods. Lately, I had seen him studying in the library — books on chemistry, biology, poetry, mythology — and was sure my roommate was trying to find more words for "sex." I'm not saying that playing Scrabble by myself on Saturday night was less pathetic, but I thought these "winter rules" were sad and dangerous and would make him miserable. I got so lost in these thoughts that I failed to realize that Rich was no longer in front of me.

Fitler Hall was the northernmost building on campus, the last thing before the sign that said:

NOW ENTERING

ENDLESS MOUNTAINS STATE FOREST

NO DOGS

NO SMOKING

NO SNOWMOBILES

Smoking was prohibited because of the danger of forest fires. Though by the end of my time at Hale, kids who ignored the sign and smoked in the woods were nevertheless careful about not flicking their matches or cigarettes into the Skulking River, imagining the whole thing might flare up like gasoline and blow the Hale School to hell.

I had never been in the woods at night and had never seen this sign posted on the other side of the ENDLESS MOUNTAINS sign.

NO HUNTING BEYOND THIS POINT

Hale's colors are blue and orange: a navy blue strangely paired with a garish, almost blinding orange. I realized for the first time that forcing our track team and our cross-country ski team and our many other teams to wear these colors, and encouraging all students to wear these colors, was a subtle way of keeping us from getting shot.

The moon came out from behind a cloud and I thought I heard a voice. Rich had a habit of talking to himself — doing his homework aloud because a thing that might be clear and beautiful in his head would look muddied, ugly on the page. He talked to himself in the shower and while sitting alone in the dining hall. He might even forget that I was in the room and say things he wanted to say to Thomasina but was too afraid to write. Things so simple as to be heartbreaking: "Hey, it's me," "You were right," "Turns out sprite can be a girl."

"Rich?" I said. The cold and the NO HUNTING sign and the creaking of the trees were freaking me out and I no longer cared about getting caught by him. The mountains north of Hale are one of the few places on the East Coast where you can still see the Milky Way, and the difference between the sky here and the sky in Philadelphia was like the difference between looking in a kaleidoscope and looking in a bowl of milk.

The door to Dr. Goltz's apartment swung open and his wife stepped outside and peered up at our window. Mrs. Goltz may have heard me bonging down the fire escape and may have heard me say Rich's name. Or the guys who lived next to Rich and me had seen him walk into the woods and had been jabbering about where he could be going, and she heard them through the pipes. Rich cruised all the time and bragged about hiking to the diner on Route 6, or the Mennonite grocery store where they didn't lock the windows at night and you could reach in and steal rock candy on a stick.

Mrs. Goltz went inside and turned off their bedroom light. She was a light sleeper and would probably hear me if I climbed back up to my room. Mrs. Goltz believed that getting boys in trouble was for their own good. Better to bust them for things like smoking and cruising before they moved on to hard drugs and hitchhiking. Although the thing that scared me most about her was making brownies with black beans instead of chocolate. Mrs. G knew the salty, fried food at the Ratty could be inedible and was only trying to give us a bit of protein. But something about her act of kindness inspired rampant cruelty. Boys began to make brownies out of things far worse than beans, while Rich was inspired to play a cruel trick on me. One night I skipped dinner to sit in my room and read the Scrabble dictionary.

"Sure," I said when Rich asked if I'd like some ice cream.

"And do you want whipped cream?"

"Sure."

I wolfed down a huge bite of white and my throat began to burn and I realized that Rich had given me a shaving cream sundae.

I walked along the edge of the woods to see if I could run around to Fitler's front door. Dr. Goltz sat hunched at the desk in his office — the extra bedroom where other faculty couples put their children — and while he was famous for not looking up from his microscope when boys walked by his window, Fitler's front door creaked on its hinges. One or both Goltzes would stumble out of their apartment and hear me running up the stairs. Now that I was out the best thing to do was wait until morning.

I walked into the woods and came across an old, rotten stretch of railroad track. Rich skulked around these woods a lot — to smoke, to drink, and, I feared, to meet Thomasina. He found old campfires and was always finding clues to Hale's early history. One time he came back with a rusty railroad spike. He gave it to Dr. Goltz, who struck it with a hammer, analyzed the flakes, and said something that blew our minds: Rich's find was more than two hundred years old, or *older than railroads*.

"Dude," Rich said, "that's impossible."

Dr. Goltz shrugged and gave Rich the book *The Johnstown Flood*. This was, in fact, a book of poems by Rich's father — one of which was about the early days of coal mining, when men were used to haul the coal cars through the mines. Rich threw it on my bed the way he would the *Derrick*'s crossword puzzle and other things that baffled him. Except for the title, the book made no mention of Johnstown or the flood. But it had a poem about the river that used to catch fire near the Urlachers' house in northeast Ohio, a poem about Centralia, and a lot of poems named for towns in Pennsylvania.

"So what does it mean?" Rich said. "Does it say about the spike?"

"It's your father's book," I said.

"Right," Rich said, "which is why I'm asking you what it means."

"I don't know. I think it means we're near an old coal mine."

I followed the railroad tracks until they were just rotten ties, and followed these ties until I came to a road. I listened for footsteps but all I could hear was the pounding of my heart. Like sex, like smoking, like a lot of things that could have given our lives meaning, driving was not absolutely forbidden for the boys of the Hale School — just damned near impossible. You had to be a senior and had to be on the honor roll. You had to find a way to get to the driver's education classes at the public high school that was seven miles away — Hale would not give you a ride — and you had to find a way to get back before sign-in. You had to actually pass the test, and then you had to convince your parents that you needed a car to get around a part of Pennsylvania with deer, mudslides, black ice, and, now, the tanker trucks that brought the millions of gallons of water needed to flush natural gas out of the wells surrounding Hale. Boys had cars as recently as the '80s, but driving had died out like a language that no one spoke anymore. Mr. Urlacher had been one of the last boys with a license and a car — a VW Bug that he drove to see his girlfriend in Ohio — and told me today's kids were in a Catch-22. We would never drive because none of us had cars to drive the rest of us to driver's ed.

"Except Thomasina."

Mr. U blushed and held up his hands in a gesture of surrender — as if I should apply the cuffs. "So you like her, too?" he said. "Too" could mean in addition to his son, or in addition to him, but I let it drop because I didn't want to know.

I stepped on a Styrofoam coffee cup. The crunch was unmistakable, and it set my teeth on edge. I was a few miles away from the Hale campus now, but this crunch meant I might still be on the right track. After cruising, Rich would climb back in our window with a small cup of coffee and would even give me some if I was awake. The cup was identical to the cups in the Ratty and Rich carried it as a prop — as if he was just coming home from an early breakfast. Sour, soapy coffee usually meant that Rich had walked to a diner or a truck stop. Viennese with cinnamon meant that Thomasina had brought him coffee in the woods. "A man camp," he said the time he came back with a shot of Jim Beam.

"A what?" I said.

Rich claimed that he had met some roughnecks at a restaurant and that these men had just arrived from Texas and had nowhere to live. They had pitched their tents in a field behind the restaurant and bathed in the Skulking and had even set up a small firing range in preparation for hunting season. One guy had a crossbow and was under the impression that Pennsylvania let people shoot bears with bows for a few days each November. Rich's trip to this "man camp" sounded like a lie to me — a daydream inspired by one of his father's poems — though Rich did not scare easily and had probably seen much stranger things in the woods. He had a fresh cut on his cheek and fingered it while talking about how to shoot a crossbow. But it looked to me like Rich had been attacked with a twig.

I walked along this road for a long time and seemed to be heading up into the mountains. I saw more coffee cups and a few beer bottles and soon saw a gleaming trail of oil or slime that led to the back of a tanker truck. CAUTION: ENVIRONMENTALLY SENSITIVE CARGO a sign on its tank said. I had read enough Orwell and seen enough of Pennsylvania to know that saying "environmentally sensitive" probably meant "toxic" and that I should be careful not to get the stuff on my shoes. Several other signs were stuck to the back of the truck — the shockingly bright reds and blues of poisonous frogs.

I kept walking and came to a diner where Rich sat across from his father. Rich drank a Coke or a root beer while his father sat with clear water in a mason jar. Mr. U had his son's mud-brown eyes, and over the last few weeks he'd acquired purple bags as if he rarely slept and frown lines around his mouth. I was about to walk in when Mr. U produced a second mason jar from his coat and put it on the table. Brownish liquid swirled and had a foamy light brown head. It looked like a jar of beer. The poet mimed taking a sip of this brownish stuff, and Rich just stared at him, as if to say, "I dare you."

Mr. U seemed like the kind of writer who could not stand the world and might have weird phobias about food and beverages. Composition 101 was a mind-boggling mix of the big, the small, and the downright bizarre. One day he would ask us to write poetry without using nouns or verbs. The next day he would tell us about the quirks of famous novelists — Proust who plugged his ears with cotton and newspaper, Melville who pulled the blinds and wrote all day and would not touch food until evening, a whole school of English poets who drank their own urine. Maybe Mr. U brewed his own beer and brought it to drink in restaurants.

I went in. The two of them were deep in conversation and did not look up at me. Both mason jars had lids, and if the brown was beer then the clear could be moonshine. I grabbed a couple of newspapers and sat in a corner booth and had been holding one paper in front of my face for several minutes, peering over the top and trying to read Mr. U's lips, when the paper brushed my nose and I recognized the smell of the *Derrick*. Some guys sniffed this paper for the slight buzz they got off the ink. I sniffed it because the smell made me sneeze and something about sneezing — the rush of blood to my brain — made me think about sex. The *Derrick* was mostly ads for sheds and drilling equipment and used cars and trucks. The classified section did not distinguish between different kinds of ads, so that an ad for a Ford Mustang ran near an ad for some actual horses, and I couldn't tell if a "rathole rig" was a truck, a well, a shed, or something else entirely.

Rich and his dad remained deep in conversation and didn't seem to see me sitting in my corner booth. The front page of the paper had an article about the Hale School for Boys leasing most of its land in the Endless Mountains to Dark Oil & Gas. Eleven wells had been fracked to date and Dark had plans to frack fifty or sixty more. I tried to read this article but my eyes could not stay with the words and I could not concentrate. Playing so much Scrabble had damaged me in several ways. I played so many weird words and was so competitive that I was always scaring off other kids in Philadelphia. I had read the dictionary from A-to-Z one summer, thinking I would learn a lot of new Scrabble words, and while I swear I read it all, I went into a trance around D or E and don't remember most of it. Worst of all was that I found myself reading books the way I read a Scrabble board — top to bottom as much as left to right. Reading vertically makes it hard to be surprised by the ending of a story or a book. I might be hanging on an author's every word but my eyes would travel down the page and read the last sentence first. I skipped over the details about Dark failing to seal some of its wells properly, and about wastewater being dumped in the Skulking, and went straight to the bottom where I learned that Richard Urlacher had written this article.

"Do you like it?" Rich said, sitting down across from me with the brown mason jar. The foam had settled down and I saw bright orange flakes floating in the murk. "You shouldn't be out like this. You don't have permission."

"And you do?"

Rich reached across the table and fingered his name in the paper. He'd probably memorized every word on this page, but I also wondered if Rich read better when reading his own writing, or reading about himself, and if he'd been asking me for help with his homework not so much because he had dyslexia, but because I was a fool and desperate to be liked by him.

"I am here to interview the poet laureate," he said, nodding to his dad. "What is your excuse for being out at night?" he said.

"I was bored."

Rich shook his head. "Her favorite thing about you is that you are unboreable." "Her" could only mean one thing at Hale and I flushed with pleasure.

"What is in that jar?" I said.

"Just something for Scrabble."

"What?"

Rich laughed and I thought I saw his father crack a smile. Rich was always teasing me about the spellings of certain Scrabble words — words like "cwm" and "qat" and "crwth" — and about words whose meanings were ridiculous. So saying a jar of muck with hairy orange flakes was part of a Scrabble game seemed like more mockery. "What's it really for?" I said.

"Proof that hydrofracturing is going to make us sick," he said.

"Where'd you get it?"

"From Dad's pond. The surface has this skin like when you burn soup. The skin dries into flakes and the flakes get all hairy, and I'm thinking Goltz can show that this stuff is poisonous."

"Can your dad give us a ride back to campus? I don't want to get caught."

"No," Rich said.

"Why not?" I said. "Because I'll embarrass you?"

"No," Rich said, "because he walked. Dad's place is less than a mile from here." I picked up the paper and tried to hide my face before Rich could read my mind, but he was too quick for me. "Don't even think about following him," he said.

"I'm — I'm just . . ." I stammered, stared at the swirling brown jar and thought it was a good metaphor for my soul. I wanted his girlfriend and wanted to bask in his father's fame. I wanted to cruise like him and, if I got caught, wanted him to save me from getting kicked out of Hale. Rich scrunched up his face and seemed amazed that Winston Crwth could be at a loss for words. Our relationship was based on the fact that I thought he had everything, while he thought I had the one thing that mattered: I could read and remember much of what I read. We were always trying to prove ourselves to each other — each guy trying to beat the other guy at his game — and it wasn't until I disobeyed him and followed his father home that I saw why his life was hell.

Rich was rapt. He could have listened to me stammering all night. Mr. U slid his chair back and stood up from his table, pushing with his elbows like someone struggling up and out of a swimming pool. He smiled and I was about to smile back when I saw his eyes were blank and I realized the man was just smiling to himself.

"So time for us to go?" I said.

"Goltz will think I've been working at the *Derrick* all night," Rich said. "So no offense, but I think your best bet is to wait till the sun comes up, then let him hear you on the fire escape."

"Can't you get me a job on the paper, too?" I said.

"As what?"

"The Scrabble Kid."

"So write about Scrabble?"

"Yes."

"I could get you a job," Rich said, "but not before morning."

"Thanks," I said.

Rich tucked the mason jar into his coat and got up and left me with the dregs of his Coke. I drank the rest of it and crunched the ice cubes with my teeth. I don't know why I did this — some part of me wondered if his father really had been daring Rich to sip the brown stuff in his mason jar, and there might be some trace of the taste in his Coke. The ice cubes were cloudy and smelled slightly off to me. A bit like rust and a bit like rotten eggs.

I watched Rich walk away and watched the road get littered

with one more cigarette. It was almost five thirty in the morning and I wouldn't get back to campus until six, after which kids could set foot outside their dorms, so I went after his dad. The road heading up into the Endless Mountains was smeared with mud and you could make out lots of footprints. You know your boots are new when even a kid from Philadelphia can track you through the woods. I followed Mr. Urlacher's tracks to a stream and saw them on the other side, wet and glistening in the dark. I could hear the smack and suck of his boots up ahead but didn't look up in case he felt me looking at his back.

I followed these sucking sounds up and over a hill and saw Mr. Urlacher walking through a gray square that looked like this:

Fracking sites, for the most part, do not look like Scrabble tiles. I'd never seen a well up close and the image of the I was the first that came to mind. Both are square and both can be a pale shade of brown that looks gray at night. The grass around this field was the same garish shade as the grass around Fitler and must have been painted, too. Walking on, I saw the thing that looked like I was a derrick and the 1 was a pipe. I know more about fracking now — the water in two dorms would become flammable, and the boys in both dorms would blame their headaches, nausea, and bad grades on fracking chemicals — but truly I was lost in my own little world if my first reaction on seeing this well was noticing the ways in which it looked like a Scrabble tile.

Rich had said his father lived just a mile away, but we must have walked two or three miles before we came to his house — a great big stone thing with a view of the Skulking. Mr. U stomped the mud off his boots and opened the front door and sang out cheerfully. I knew he was divorced but thought he might have a pet, or might have his son's habit of talking to himself. Mr. U walked into the house and then sang out something else. The back door banged open and I heard several thumps — Mr. U drumming on the side of a big white plastic tub.

The front door was open and I now found my legs taking me toward the house. I walked through the front door and told myself I would get a quick look at his library. But of course the first thing that caught my eye was a Scrabble board. I was reading the first word to be played in this game — DRINK, with the K on a double-letter score and the whole word doubled for a score of thirty — when I heard footsteps and saw the voluptuous lips of Thomasina Wodtke-Weir. She wore jeans and shoes but her shirt was inside out.

"Win," Thomasina said, "what the hell are you doing here?"

"We need a third person for our Scrabble club," I said stupidly.

"And you want me?"

"Yes," I said, "to make it official. Is this where Rich comes at night? To play Scrabble with you and Mr. Urlacher?" Bubbling up in my brain were the many, many problems with finding her in his house in the middle of the night. But I've always been the kind of person who can solve only one problem at a time.

"No," she said, "Rich got some job at the local newspaper. Don't tell Rich you saw me here. Listen, Win, you're very sweet, but I can't join your club."

"Iss the one?" Mr. U said, slurring what sounded like "Is this the one?" He looked drunk or sick, and stood crookedly with one arm bent behind his back. His shoes and his pants were splattered with mud; he must have fallen near his fracking site because there were a few blades of fluorescent green grass on his neck. He looked like a scarecrow or a voodoo doll that'd been dragged through the mud.

"Sir, it's me, it's Winston Crwth."

"Call me Mr. U," he said. "How long have you been standing in my living room?"

"I followed Rich to the diner, and then followed you," I said. "Are you okay?"

"He's writing his masterpiece," Thomasina said, "if it doesn't kill him first."

"Don't say that—bad luck," he said. "Beer? Don't worry, I make it with water from the water buffalo."

"No, thanks. So I see she is teaching you to Scrab?"

Mr. U shrugged. I looked over their game and saw SWIVE and several other potentially dirty words, but they had been keeping score and, perhaps, not swiving. I looked at his bookshelves and saw busts and boxes and crumbling rock specimens where there should have been books. I saw the clear blue flame of Dark Oil & Gas on a framed certificate. "Mr. U, this says that you're a Dark Scholar, too?"

"Sure," he said, "Thomasina helped me with the paperwork."

"But that hardly seems fair," I said. "Doesn't Dark use that money for kids—"

"Thomasina's here because I need to coach a sport or run some kind of club. She's been teaching me to Scrab."

"Prove it," I said, and dumped their board upside down and began scooping their tiles back into the bag. Mr. U sat. He sat awkwardly, and only after playing several words did he pull the brown bottle out from behind his back—bringing the headmaster's daughter home but taking care not to drink in front of her being a good measure of Mr. U's character.

Our teacher could have won, and he probably should have

won, but our game wasn't even close. He drew both blank tiles and sat boggling at his rack, thrilled and overwhelmed by the possibilities. He rearranged his tiles and hemmed and hawed and sipped his beer but could not bring himself to part with the blanks, and was clearly waiting to play some word worthy of a poet laureate. But hard as he tried, I blocked him with EEK, SUQ, VAV, and other little, ugly words that, when read aloud, made me sound like I was choking or might have Tourette's syndrome.

"It's my fault," Thomasina said. "I taught him to play this way."

"To lose?"

"No," she said, "to play Scrabble beautifully."

23

Thomasina joined our club. Three-way Scrabble is about as boring as I'd imagine a ménage à trois to be — the clutter, the awkwardness, how hard it is to concentrate — so Thomasina, Hose, and I would take turns playing while Mr. U read, or scribbled in his notebook, or, sometimes, just sat staring into space in a corner of the Fitler common room.

I'd heard Mr. U compare writing to childbirth. And if he really was working on his masterpiece, then sitting in a chair with a blank look on his face, or a green seasick look as if the chair were bolted to the deck of a ship, could be part of his "pregnancy."

One night the sound of a soda can rumbling startled Mr. U and he yawned and reached behind his head as if trying to grab a book.

"Look at him," Thomasina said. "The man thinks he's in my house."

She'd been calling him "the man" ever since I surprised them at his house. Seventeen-year-old Thomasina had seemed like the adult that night — scolding him for drinking and scolding me for walking in without knocking — but no longer called him "Tom" and no longer pried his coffee cup from his hand when he fell asleep in the common room. Whatever had been going on between the two of them — whether Thomasina was his muse, his lover, or, however unlikely, his underage Scrabble coach — the spell had been broken and I seemed to be responsible.

Mr. U sat in a corner of the common room and slept like a kid who'd fallen asleep in a car and been transferred to his bed — with one hand on his crotch and a waffle pattern on his face. I felt bad for him, remembering my father falling asleep at the table on Sunday nights, his lap and the kitchen floor littered with thought papers.

"Can't we play in your house?" I said to Thomasina.

"If we keep three feet on the floor. And since there are four of us, three feet should be doable."

24

Of all the rules I'd broken and of all the lines I'd crossed — sneaking off campus and stepping into the quagmire of T and U's relationship — it was the simple act of talking about sex with her that got me in trouble and made Rich think I was trying to steal his girlfriend. Fitler Hall worked like a big, nonstop game of telephone. People heard things through the walls and tried to hear them through the pipes, and I hate to think what "if we keep three feet on the floor" had become by the time it got to Rich. Of course the truth was much worse — that his girlfriend had been going to his father's house — and so bad that I could not use it to defend myself.

Rich, perversely, liked to climb down our fire escape right after sign-in — flaunting the fact that he could be outside at night — and I knew something was wrong when I came back from Scrabble club and found him smoking in our room. He wore a beautiful pair of pale blue silk pajamas that had been hanging in our closet all fall — a virgin among his rough and wrinkled shirts — and had positioned his bed so that it blocked both windows. "So I'm staying in tonight."

"Oh?" I said.

"Or maybe I'll write a love letter and have you bring it to her."

"I am staying in," I said.

"Why, Win? I thought you were my friend."

"You called it. You're the one who said that Thomasina was my type."

"Don't flatter me."

"Okay," I said.

"Can I play?"

"Of course," I said, assuming he was asking if he could join our Scrabble club. I wrote down a list of all the two-letter words for him. He kept asking what they meant and I told him not to worry about meaning yet — that meaning would just slow him down.

"Can I play whatever version of Scrabble is making her fall in love with you?"

"This is it. The version where you keep score and try to win."

"But that's so boring."

"That's my life. Also, Rich, I'm pretty sure that she's not in love with me."

"No?" he said. "Then why did my dad agree to chaperone you guys so you can go to Harrisburg?"

"He did?" I said. "Rich, I don't know what Thomasina told you, but your father seems to think I can get him a meeting with . . . There's this Scrabble tournament, and apparently the winner gets —"

"Thomasina thinks that, too — I mean that you're such a freak that LaRue will meet with you. What's an ay?"

"A sloth," I said.

"Is that how you pronounce it, *ay*?"

"No," I said, "it's spelled a-i but you pronounce it *eye-ee*."

"Were you going to tell me that, or were you going to let me sound like an idiot?"

"I . . ."

But horribly, unluckily, even this made Rich think that I was making fun of him. I won't lie. I didn't think it was unlucky at the time that Rich crumpled up my list and threw it under his bed. *I win*. That's what I thought — without thinking what I'd won or how Rich would survive Hale without Thomasina. Because Dr. Weir was right. You need something, anything, to make the other kids treat you with respect.

Rich slammed our door and stormed off to smoke by himself in the bathroom. The perfect place to smoke because you could always blame someone else. Rich had a lot of bad stuff under his bed — cigarettes and a bottle of sparkling hard cider and a copy of the answers to an old SAT test — and I did not want Goltz, or whoever finally busted Rich, to find a list in my handwriting with Rich's other contraband. Rich was not a reader. But give him this, he was curious, and I found a lot of stuff far stranger than my list when I got down on my knees: a football signed by Linda King when she was Miss Northern Tier; a list of side effects for what happened if you were exposed to diesel, butane, arsenic, and about a dozen other chemicals; a book called *The War on Boys* that smelled like it had been dunked in wine; a dusty pink clam that must have been a retainer; a pile of sand that looked like the top of an anthill but was just a pile of sand; a Hale diploma with no name from 1989; an orange vest that said DARK OIL & GAS on the back; a map of the Skulking River on which Rich had drawn stick-figure cows grazing along the shore; and a crude drawing of an eight-man scull on which he had written my name in at starboard bow.

But instead of Vaughn Warnicke and Jimmy Weems and my other teammates, Rich had me rowing with seven afflictions.

Tourette's Syndrome
Winston Crwth
Yellow Eyes
Giardia
Yellow Eyes
Bad Knees
PDD-NOS
Amnesia

Now of all the crazy things under my roommate's bed, this list was the craziest, and I should have put it back ... except that I was spellbound by the sight of my own name and wanted to know why my teammates were sick and why Rich was suddenly interested in my life.

Following Rich to the diner had been so disastrous that following him into the bathroom now seemed relatively safe. Except that I walked in on him striking a match and raising the flame to his lips. "Don't!" I said. It's as if I knew what would happen next. Rich flicked the match in the sink and turned to me with his unlit cigarette dangling dumbly in his mouth.

"What's the meaning of this list? Why is everybody sick?"

"Fracking along the river."

"So the whole school is sick, or just the guys on the crew team?"

Rich shrugged. "It's actually hard to tell. Many of the symptoms of living in Fitler and living near fracking are similar."

"Why do you care?"

"I'm on deadline."

"For the *Derrick*? That's insane. Rich, you know you're writing for a fracking newspaper?"

"Not all papers are corrupt."

"No, I mean you're writing *for* the fracking industry."

"So?" Rich said. "I'll change their minds. My dad does it all the time. You know, you should see the looks on your guys' faces after you've been rowing and your shirts are frozen to —"

"We're sick because of fracking?"

"Yes. Sick just like those cows who live along the Skulking, too."

"Cows?" I said, pretending that I had not seen his map.

"There's a dairy farm between here and my dad's. I walked down one day and the lady is, like, the only person in the Endless Mountains who has not leased her land. The stuff that comes out of her tap is . . . there is no word for it . . . but her milk is undrinkable. And I find it interesting that her property ends right at Dead Man's Curve."

"You're confused. The name Dead Man comes from when they found a dead guy on the rocks in the nineteenth century."

Rich shook his head as if saddened by my ignorance. "Coach K won't let you guys row beyond Dead Man's Curve. Vaughn Warnicke told me so." We could not row around the curve for the same reason — rocks — that a floating corpse got stuck.

"How does fracking cause bad knees?" Bad knees was Vaughn Warnicke, who'd ruined them playing soccer and now walked like Frankenstein. Amnesia was Bob Peterbilt, the pitcher who'd gotten beaned and forgotten how to throw his curveball. "You know we all do crew because we got injured doing some other sport, right? Not because crew injured us. And I bet you didn't know that the guys in the engine room *all* have giardia, and that's why the whites of their eyes are yellow?"

"Giardia?"

"I'm just reading your list, Rich."

"Oh, that's right, giardia."

"They got it during a summer rowing program at our sister school in Mexico. The drugs can make it better but they turn your eyes yellow."

"Oh," Rich said, "I didn't know."

"And there's no way that Jimmy Weems has Tourette's."

"He does in Leah."

"What?" I said.

"Jimmy has Tourette's in that game he plays all day on his phone," Rich said. "The game where you pretend to be a kid in high school."

"And how come you don't say what's wrong with me?"

Rich was about to say when flames engulfed his head. A gooey black substance like burnt marshmallow ran down the wall, and Rich held his face gingerly. But the flames had shot up so quickly that they swept over Rich without really burning him . . . or so I thought until I saw his expression. He looked surprised and terrified because he was, but also because his eyebrows had been burned completely off. They never grew back and Rich would wear this stunned look for the rest of high school.

"Jesus — you okay?" I said.

Rich pointed to the match he'd lit and then dropped in the sink. "Sorry — that was an accident. I didn't say what's wrong with you because your name already sounds like a disease." Rich said this casually, as if a fireball had not just engulfed his head, making me think he'd lit Fitler's water on fire before. But he may have been in shock. He had screamed — I hadn't heard — and I must have been in shock, too, because the blare of the fire alarm in the hall seemed to come from far away, and the bongs of doom that were Dr. Goltz climbing the stairs sounded peaceful, godlike, calm, like bells at a funeral.

25

I am also to blame for what happened to Rich next. Smoking was a strike and setting things on fire — including yourself — was a strike, and I knew Rich would be kicked out if I did not get back to our room and hide his other stuff or throw it out the window.

It took five seconds for me to get from the bathroom to our room — long enough for me to start worrying about myself instead and start wondering if Fitler's flaming water meant that Ian and Trevonia Dark would take away my scholarship. My grades weren't good enough to get another scholarship. My poor father had taken out a second mortgage on our house to send me to Clovis Friends. The jobs kids did for money at other boarding schools — washing the dishes, raking the leaves, cleaning the toilets in the dorms — Hale made its kids do for free. My mother had some kind of job on a farm in Oakland but seemed to get paid in honey, fruits, and vegetables. The National Scrabble Championship, with its grand prize of $50,000, wasn't until the spring. The Pennsylvania Championship was in a few weeks, but first prize there was $500 and a chance to play a game against Linda King LaRue.

I ran to our room with every intention of saving myself and of trying to save Rich, but was a different person by the time I got there. The insane, mind-bending sight of flaming water made me feel that I had stumbled on something bigger than myself. I felt this way about Scrabble once but now saw that I'd been wrong. My list looked silly, small compared to the other things under my roommate's bed — the words so much babbling.

I had time to grab one thing before the final bong of doom — before Goltz climbed the final step and saw me with my head

stuck under my roommate's bed — and I chose Rich's crude drawing of the Skulking River. Everything else would be put in trash
bags by Goltz and, later, examined by Dr. Weir, and the evidence
against Rich was even worse than it looked: the SAT questions
were from a recent test; the label on the hard cider said NOT FOR
SALE so that Rich must have stolen it from a restaurant; the study
on the effects of butane, arsenic, and other chemicals on human
health had been stolen from Dr. Goltz's desk; some of the library
books were more than a year overdue and one of them was more
than ten years overdue; the dusty pink retainer was too small to
belong to a teenager, as if Rich had stolen a child's orthodontia.

The stuff under Rich's bed was more than enough to get him
expelled. It might even be enough to get him sent to jail. I had
seen my friend perform minor miracles and held out hope that
he would find a way to save himself. Rich attended a sad, cold
boarding school for boys in northeastern Pennsylvania, and yet
he'd had a girlfriend and an off-campus job and could go outside
at night. He figured out that the way to pass the Hale swim test
was, in fact, to sink and push off the bottom and come up for air.
He was a reporter even though reading was maddeningly hard for
him — and this, more than anything, made me think Rich shared
some of his father's genius.

26

Rich was suspended for the rest of the semester and went to live
with his father. His stuff disappeared from our room and his writing disappeared from the *Hale Mountaineer*. The RU carved into
a bathroom stall was itself vandalized until it said 88. Oddly, the
most damning thing that had been under his bed — the orange vest
that said DARK OIL & GAS — had been hung among my shirts — a
parting gift.

Rich's fire got the whole dorm in trouble with Dr. and Mrs. Goltz, and we sat chewing on her black bean brownies and not touching our cups of sugar-free apple juice while the Goltzes reminded us about the danger of smoking in our rooms and the fact that Fitler — the oldest dorm on campus — was a tinderbox. Hose was asked to send his heating coil home and Jason Moskowitz was asked to get rid of Fred, his mouse, whose little teeth could chew through a computer cord and who now terrified Dr. Goltz.

"And the water?"

"Win," Goltz said, "I'd like to give you Rich's job as proctor and fire marshal. You get a red hat and two days off each semester." Another of Rich's perks. Vacation days as if he was a school employee. Kids on the honor roll also got two days off each semester and made the rest of us miserable as they planned wild trips to the Steamtown Mall in Scranton, the Arby's in Wyomingville, the multiplex in the middle of nowhere that did not check IDs for R-rated films — all with the wild eyes and big, shit-eating grins of sailors getting off a ship. Like a lot of Hale's rules, giving days off to the kids who were, for the most part, doing swimmingly was cruel and made the rest of us feel that our lives were meaningless.

"And the water?"

No one spoke. Hale was full of things that I did not understand — I still don't understand how I actually went to classes on Saturdays — and it was too much to ask the other guys in Fitler to believe that our water was a fire hazard, too.

"I know what I saw," I said. "Do you think you're going to buy my silence with two days off from school?"

"I do."

I used the first day to sleep until twelve thirty — the best sleep I'd ever had — then get to crew practice early so I could take a single out and row up the Skulking and look for Rich's cows. I'd never rowed a single scull and couldn't keep it straight for long and gave up when I hit a rock. Unlike rowing in an eight — a maddening exercise in trying to keep your body in sync with the herking, jerking bodies of seven other big galoots — rowing a single is an exercise in keeping your body in sync with your herking, jerking thoughts. Thinking *left* made me veer left and thinking *right* made me veer right, and the trick seemed to be thinking with my back, my legs, my arms — to try not to think in words.

Coach K had a cheap cell phone and could only call his parents in Russia for a few minutes at a time and only if he walked around with the phone held out in front of him like a dowser, searching for a signal — a search that could leave him standing on a stump, on the fender of an old, abandoned car, in the water, if it meant keeping his connection. Today he stood on the dock, speaking into his phone like it was a tin can in a game of telephone. He was smiling and seemed thrilled to be talking to his father, a man whose slow, slurred voice sounded like a swarm of bees — his Ss so slow that they sounded more like Zs. This voice buzzed as I came in and climbed out of my scull, the oarlocks pitching wildly and slamming into the dock. And as if my bad technique were audible in Russia, the voice grew louder, angrier. Coach K grabbed my shoulder and pushed me slightly to the left. Then he pushed me back a step. "Excellent," he said, and winked.

I had spent hundreds of hours being yelled at by Coach K, pulling on my oar until my chest felt like it was on fire, and my first compliment was for standing still, doing nothing, while Coach K's father yelled at him.

"Winston — you make excellent human antenna."

"Can I talk?"

"You talk," he said. "This is speech I hear before."

"Can I row past Dead Man's Curve?"

"Not in hunting season, no."

"I'm supposed to find the cows."

"The cause?"

"The cows."

"Winston Crwth" — he tore through my name like nobody else at Hale, his big, Russian jaw chewing up the consonants — "you need to learn to keep your eyes in the boat."

The school paper said nothing about Rich's accident. A black chunk of shale disappeared from a shelf in the back of Goltz's classroom where he kept oddities — a piece of aa that looked like a sponge, a spider trapped in amber, a piece of pahoehoe that looked painfully sharp, and a sprinkling of pyrite that had been panned from the Skulking and then used as fool's gold. Kids borrowed these things all the time and did not put them back; the suspicious thing was that Goltz stopped saying "shale" as well and began talking about the land under Hale as "the Marcellus" instead of "the Marcellus shale." "The Marcellus is what's left of the soup — the fish and krill and microorganisms — that lived in the ocean that was Pennsylvania." And instead of "fracking" Goltz began to talk about "hydraulic fracturing." The "man camps" where roughnecks lived were now "company towns," and "Dark" became "Dark Oil and Gas," a name just as sinister. Goltz no longer challenged me when I said things like "granites for ingrates" or "diorites for idiots," and, in general, seemed to be proposing a truce. He would let me wreck parts of his lectures with my idiotic comments and I would let the frackers wreck Pennsylvania.

The sounds were everywhere in those days: the distant pounding of the drills, the grinding of the bulldozers and the thrilling chink when they bit into a rock, the gunning of the engine on this one kind of truck that made kids duck every time — a sound like a biplane coming to gun us down. Hale had leased the drilling rights to much of its land and had every reason to hide what had happened to Rich. And for a long time Hale's response to the evidence that fracking might be making kids sick was to throw up its hands and say, "So does boarding school."

The really disconcerting thing was that Rich was silent about the fire, too. He kept writing for the *Derrick* and profiled some of next year's Dark Scholars. Even now, even when I was desperate for evidence, I could not take Rich's writing seriously and almost failed to see that, between his profile of an eighth grade girl who had won a spelling bee and a Dark Scholarship, and his Q&A with a twelfth grade boy who had run for mayor of a coal town in central Pennsylvania, was a feature on his dad. Proof that the poet laureate of Pennsylvania was competing with children for handouts from Dark Oil & Gas. Mr. U looked younger and happier in the photograph. And he sounded different. He talked about the joys of working with young people and claimed to be writing the great American fracking poem. "Sort of like *Moby-Dick* except with fracking instead of whales."

Rich did not answer my emails or my text messages. I would get strange, garbled texts and would hope these were him — that Rich had sat on his phone or typed things by accident — but they were for Howard Crow, the man who last summer was getting my phone calls. All the evidence under Rich's bed had vanished and all four of the library's books about fracking were still checked out in his name. The black marshmallowy stuff — a mixture of burnt soap, burnt paint, and burnt shaving cream — had been scraped off the bathroom walls. Goltz refused to talk about the fire or say the word "fracking," and I began to feel the whole world was against me. Even JANE did something odd — or something that seemed to go against her nature. Hose, the first time we met, told me Dark had been fracking in Texas and Oklahoma since the '50s. "That's how Dark knows it's safe." JANE could not challenge words, but neither could she bluff; and I knew that whatever Dark had been doing in the past was not like fracking in Pennsylvania because no matter what I did, no matter how many times I played RACK with the R below or to the right of a triple-word-score square, JANE would CRACK, TRACK, and WRACK, but she would refuse to FRACK.

27

I thought we'd have nowhere to row once the Skulking froze and would just splash around the swimming pool the way we did at Clovis Friends. But Coach K thought differently. Thanks to Dark the school bought ten new ergometers—rowing machines that look like big black insects—and Coach K gave us the choice of rowing on the icy Skulking or strapping ourselves to one of these praying mantises.

At first, I was the only one who chose the river, and I would flop around until my scull was full of chunks of ice and water and I had to turn back. I thought Coach K would approve, but I was so bad and my scull tipped so violently that he couldn't bear to watch. He would sit in the bus, his breath fogging up the window until I couldn't see his face, just the hulking torso of the Headless Bus Driver.

The weather turned brutally cold in late November and the Skulking would freeze over at night and only be rowable for a few hours in the middle of the day. Flailing with my little oars and trying not to fall in made me so hot, so frantic, my ears burning from the cold, my face from embarrassment, that *everything* seemed hot to me. Thin, dark ice looked like the burnt skin on some Ratty casserole. Coach K attached a blade—an icebreaker—to the front of my scull, and I loved the fact that he never asked why I was doing this to myself, as if this was no crazier than rowing in an eight. I was trying to row farther in my single than we'd ever rowed together—trying to get around Dead Man's Curve and see whatever Rich had seen. Looking back, the smart thing would have been to walk to Mr. U's, which was several miles upstream, and just come down in a raft. And this way I would have spared Vaughn his fracking calamity.

Vaughn had stopped asking me if I needed "to talk" and had stopped sitting with me at dinner because I now seemed like I had it made, having taken Rich's place as the only guy at Hale eating dinner with a girl. Vaughn had the smooth stroke and the freak-ishly long arms of a guy with a legitimate shot at rowing in the Olympics. But his greatest ambition was to have a girlfriend. Rich and Vaughn were the two guys I knew who'd lost their virginity. Rich did it with a girl from Wyomingville, whom he met while working the late shift at the *Derrick*, and Rich said it cleared up his skin and helped him get some of the references in his father's poetry. Vaughn just shook his head and got the lost, hurt look that rowers get after they pull too hard, too fast, and catch a humili-ating crab. Based on the frustrations of my own sex life — which consisted entirely of dreams in which I'd be having sex but stop because I was afraid the girl would get pregnant — I liked to think the whole thing got less frustrating, less miserable, once you finally *did it*. But doing it only made Vaughn more miserable.

I found a better map of the Skulking in the library and cal-culated that, if I left in the morning, I could row to Dead Man's Curve, and maybe as far as Rich's fracked dairy farm, and be back for dinner. I had already submitted my request to take my second day off, and had already packed a lunch and walked to the boat-house, when I saw Coach K sitting in a pile of wood and metal that had been the rigging and the inside of my scull.

"I need that."

"Tomorrow," he said, "after it's been winterized. Win, you know you row the way my father rode a horse. Like a man pursued by demons. What has gotten into you?"

I got my roommate suspended and I think the Skulking is making everybody sick, I thought. "I don't know," I said. "It's hard to say. I just need to row. Can I take the double out?"

"I'm too strong for you," he said.

"I'll get Vaughn."

"I need him fresh."

"Let me take Vaughn out in a double and I'll tell you how to pass the Hale swim test."

Coach K grinned. "I passed," he said.

"How?"

"By struggling violently. Winston, I'll make you a deal. Stay here for winter break and practice in the tanks."

"Coach," I said, "a deal is where you give me something in return."

"Like?"

"I need to be able to get out of my dorm at night."

"*Nyet.* Only the swimming coach is that powerful. Stay here for winter break and I'll let you and Vaughn row around Dead Man's Curve."

"Where do I sleep?" A kid from Taiwan had spent Thanksgiving with the Wodtke-Weirs, sleeping in a bedroom next to Thomasina's. Winter break was three weeks long and I weighed the idea of sloshing around the tanks, listening to Coach K bark, against the warmth of my father's couch in Philadelphia.

"You sleep in your dorm, of course. I'm not sure Fitler's heat has an off switch anyway."

I'd been harboring wild thoughts about visiting Thomasina over winter break — thinking the school's prudish rules about sex would be relaxed or, better yet, unenforceable — and doubted I could convince her, Dr. Weir, and Mr. U that I needed to be here for Scrabble club.

28

Vaughn sat in the front row of Rocks for Jocks. I waited until Goltz had his back to the class and walked right up to Vaughn and dropped the orange Dark Oil & Gas vest on his desk.

"What is this?"

"Crew team winter rules," I said. "Coach K gave us permission so long as we don't get shot."

Vaughn turned the vest over with a look like a Scrabbler hoping for a good tile and frowned at the sight of DARK. "But didn't this belong to Rich?" he said. "And what are you going to wear?"

I told Vaughn the land beyond Dead Man's Curve was fracked and that we would not be shot. He refused to get up until class was over — the difference between him and me — so that I now spent an hour of my day off listening to Goltz's dumb mnemonics for the periodic table. Pb was lead because peanut butter feels like lead in your gut. Radon was Rn because the stuff is poisonous and can make you need a nurse.

"And Ru?" I challenged him. "Is there an easy way to remember Richard Urlacher?"

Goltz said something about Babe Ruth and ruthenium, but I didn't really hear because I was suddenly furious with him for disappearing Rich. Frivolous as Rich seemed — with his pink shirts, sloppy texts, and clove cigarettes — he had been nice to me, and, too late, I understood that this guy who could barely read was a kindred spirit.

29

Vaughn wore the orange vest and I chattered noisily. Vaughn also wore shorts and I saw the long, jagged scars where his knees had been put back together with staples and titanium. "Aren't you cold?"

"The bigger problem is airport security. I tried traveling with X-rays but the inside of my left knee even *looks* like a bomb."

Vaughn had always wanted to row beyond Dead Man's Curve—the edge of the flat earth on which the crew team lived—and yet his head stayed ramrod straight as we rowed around the curve and he kept going back and forth as if he were in the tanks, staring at the bricks in Dreissegacker's basement. He grunted at the catch, the beginning of a stroke, and puffed at the finish, and his whole body flinched when one of our oarlocks dipped and got a little wet. "Vaughn, you understand that Coach K isn't here?" I said.

"Nnn," he said.

My bad form rocked the boat and made it hard for him to speak, impossible for him to turn his head and see what I could see: a barbed wire fence on one side of the river and a sign that said NO TRESPASSING. All Vaughn cared about was keeping the boat level, straight—an obsession with form that blinded him to the rocks, the chunks of ice, the Styrofoam coffee cup that caught on an oarlock and created a slight drag, which Vaughn seemed to blame on me. Of course I was even worse, not bothering to row well *or* turn around and look for dangers up ahead, and this is how I failed to see the boy with the BB gun until he had shot Vaughn in the back of the neck.

"Ow," Vaughn said, and slapped his neck, but got his hand back on his oar in time for his next stroke. The boy was pumping his gun for another shot, and I actually thought it might be easier to call out a power ten and row the hell away from him than get Vaughn's attention. He was bleeding. The BB looked like a zit under his skin. But like a mule or some other dumb animal, he pulled harder for the pain.

"Vaughn!"

"Not now."

"You were shot," I said.

Vaughn turned his head and saw the kid with the BB gun and leaned back and performed a feat of extraordinary strength and stupidity — grabbing me by the arms and rolling the scull so that we fell into the freezing river, the water so cold that it took my breath away. The scull rolled up on its side — a heaving wooden wave that might crash down on our heads, but which, for the moment, was keeping us from being shot.

"Kid?" I yelled. "We're actually —"

A pop, a splintering, and a small hole in the hull.

"Jesus Christ — he shot the boat," Vaughn said.

"Young man?" I said. The *chunk-a-chunk* of the gun being pumped. My feet were deep in cold mud and my penis bobbed in my shorts like a piece of ice.

"Kid, we're here to help!" I said.

"Get off our land, you fracking freaks."

Vaughn took off the vest and threw it ashore in a gesture of surrender. "It's fine," he said, "we're actually not with Dark Oil and Gas." Vaughn's lips were turning blue and his arms were trembling from trying to hold the scull up in front of us.

"That is what the last man said." He shot Vaughn in the chest, but this time the BB bounced and plopped harmlessly in the river. Vaughn let go of the boat and crossed his arms and stared at him, and the boy, discouraged, turned and aimed his gun at me.

"We're from Hale," I said, and raised my hands above my head. "We just came because the same problems you've been having with your farm —"

"Get off our land, you prep school freaks."

The boat was drifting away and taking on water fast, and all three of us watched as it headed for a rock. Vaughn walked after it, the water rising to his neck. The kid lowered his gun and I heard his teeth chattering, and I suddenly realized that, long before fracking and long before Dark got the rights to everything along this river — except for this kid's property — boys from the Hale School must have been stealing his family's milk and tipping his family's cows and rowing beyond Dead Man's Curve to look for comely milkmaids.

"It's for Scrabble."

Vaughn said this. A damning thing to say if it got back to Dr. Weir. I was too cold to think and too scared to move and just stared in amazement as Vaughn hauled himself into the boat, hoisting his legs over the side like big, frozen logs. "This is Win. We call him that because he's such a loser. He plays this game called Scrabble —"

"I know what Scrabble is," the kid said, and aimed the gun at him.

"Good," Vaughn said, "then maybe you can show him the proper way to play."

Vaughn rowed away with the boat riding alarmingly low in the river — a short, quick stroke to try to keep the whole thing from sinking. Vaughn was tough as hell and even the kid seemed impressed by the spectacle of this shivering blue guy rowing a double by himself.

The kid held out a branch, the bark curled up like paper. "So what are you?" he said, and pulled me out of the river. "Some kind of pariah?"

"You could say that —"

"I just did."

"Hale is my third high school in the last three years," I said. "I love girls but the only one at Hale has a crush on one of my teachers. I'm really good at Scrabble but most people think Scrabble is ridiculous. So I have problems, too."

"Is it true that you guys go to school on Saturdays?"

"I got a day off for being my dorm's fire marshal but I'm spending it with some kid with a gun on me."

The kid gave me his hat and may have saved me from Vaughn's fate — double pneumonia, a trip to the hospital, and winter break in California. He led me to his house and asked me if I was a large or an extra large, and I had to laugh when he brought out a box of Hale crew paraphernalia: a thick wool turtleneck and all kinds of T-shirts and tank tops, one of which was so small that it would look like a bra on me and would look like a very skimpy bra on Vaughn; a complete set of eight tank tops from some school whose name began with E; a megaphone that could be strapped to a barking coxswain's face to make him look like a dog; a cracked, pitted piece of foam that may have come from one of the rubber balls Coach K stuck on the bows of our boats; a piece of black leather that looked innocent enough at the bottom of the box, but which, when I held it up, looked like chaps, a mask, a gag.

"What is this?"

"You tell me," he said. "Maybe some sort of sick sex thing?"

"It's for sitting —"

"The wrestling team wears Saran Wrap under their clothes," the kid said thoughtfully, "so maybe —"

I put it back. The black thing had straps and may have been worn on guys' butts. The box was also full of trash and the kid already seemed to think that I was a freak. "Where are all your cows?" I said. "Isn't this a dairy farm?"

"We're all out of milk," he said. "Do you want some Diet Coke?"

"Are they sick?"

"Their milk will make you sick. My dad tried to sell them but people don't want the meat." The kid got up and turned on the kitchen sink. He filled a glass and held the stuff up to his nose.

"Are you lying?"

"What?" I said.

"About working for Dark Oil. Because that other guy who came here said he worked for a newspaper. What he didn't say was that it was a fracking newspaper."

"I'm not lying."

"No?" he said. "Because the water's clean today. Usually, it's like jelly but it gets better every time we complain—better for about a week."

I was a Dark Scholar and the guy whose map I followed to this farm worked for the *Derrick* and my English teacher was a Dark scholar, too. "I . . ." I said. "I'm going to play in this Scrabble tournament. Apparently, the winner gets to meet with Linda King LaRue."

"Give her this," the kid said, and opened the door of his refrigerator. Jars and jars of water, some of which shimmered in the sunlight streaming into the fridge, some of which, suspiciously, seemed to suck up the light. The kid chose a jar that looked clean enough, but the stuff, when he turned it upside down, defied gravity and clung to the top.

"I'm . . . Kid, I may not be the best messenger."

"Deliver it. That's different."

"Don't your neighbors—"

"They don't care. They're the ones who gave Dark the right to drill here. My dumb dad didn't sign a lease—"

"Don't call your father dumb," I said.

"—because he didn't understand that they drill *sideways* and that we would still be fracked."

I shut up because the kid had cracked a jar and was trying to pour me a glass of water. The stuff that flopped out was clear and glistened like a jellyfish. Quickly, he rescrewed the lid as if more could flop out by itself, the lid spinning so that I read

818

as "infinity divided by infinity" before reading it as "818," the impossibly high score I'd seen in Leah's Scrabble set. "Suite Code eight-eighteen," I read off the label on the jar. "Does not contain significant amounts of barium, calcium, iron, potassium, magnesium, manganese, sodium, or strontium. What is this?"

"Our test results, saying that our water's fine."

The "D" who got 818 as his Scrabble score in Leah, or who wrote it as his score, was a cheat, a liar, and I felt these test results must also be fraudulent. "I'll give this to LaRue," I said.

30

The boat sank before Vaughn could row it back to the boathouse. Vaughn then swam ashore and stumbled to a drill site and got the guys to give him a ride to the hospital with frostbite on eight toes and the BB in his neck. The word about the shooting got around quickly and I knew things were serious when I opened my door to find Thomasina's father sitting on my floor. Dr. Weir sat in the exact spot where Rich's bed used to be, sitting the way you would on a bed, as if he could not accept my room's new reality.

"Did you guess it?"

"What?" I said.

"Don't play games with me," Dr. Weir said. "My daughter has aa and . . ." He held my list of Scrabble words up to the light. "And about seven or eight of these other things. Win, you understand this way of playing is forbidden?"

"Yes."

"Why?" he said. "I want to hear you say why it is forbidden."

"Because kids might do the verbs?"

"Take those off."

I'd tromped back in the kid's wool socks and his father's galoshes, but I couldn't feel my feet and was so tired that I just stared at the water trickling through a hole and pooling in a crack between two ripped, rubbery sections of my floor — a potato bug rising on this tide and spinning slowly, lifelessly.

"Who gave you permission to row around Dead Man's Curve?"

"I am not a rat," I said.

"Who gave you —"

"Coach Kashvilinski." I broke this easily, but in the same way that Vaughn kept rowing with a hole in his scull, a BB in his neck, his shoes somewhere in the river, and the knowledge he was doomed, something about Hale had taught me to tell the truth. "But please don't punish Vaughn," I said. "The river could be on fire and he wouldn't turn his head."

"You're saying he didn't know that you'd rowed around the curve? That he wasn't posing as an employee of Dark Oil —"

"Right," I said, "because the Dark logo is only on the back."

"The Feldkirchers —"

"Who?" I said.

"You blew right by the signs saying that you might be shot and you went into his home when his ten-year-old son was there and these people have a name."

"They have this," I said, handing him the sticky jar from the Feldkirchers' fridge.

"You stole this?"

I shook my head. "I told the kid I'd give it to Linda King LaRue."

Weir's nostrils flared the way his daughter's did when she got angry, and he made a strange sound like someone trying to say "yes" and "no" simultaneously. "You're telling me you have a meeting with the governor?"

"Yes," I said. A true statement if I won the tournament.

"You and Mr. Urlacher?"

"No, just me and her," I said.

"A meeting about fracking?"

"Yes."

My family had some clout in Harrisburg — my grandfather had been friendly with several state senators and had briefly been the senate parliamentarian — and Rich had been hiding a lot of damning things under his bed. But the thing that seemed to scare Weir most was the water in the jar. "Winston, I want you to know how sorry I am — how sorry we all are — about Rich's accident. And we're going to make sure that nothing like that ever happens again. Fitler's pipes will be replaced and we'll get you connected to the rest of the school. And until we do we'll get you a water buffalo. But I have to tell you that fracking's not my biggest fear. My biggest fear is that you love language but don't seem to understand that words have meaning. Hale is the oldest boarding school in this part of the state and this is not the first time a headmaster has been told that the sky is falling. Tell me you care about fracking and care about the facts and I will drive you to Harrisburg myself. But what I won't tolerate is going as a joke and making Linda King LaRue think your meeting is some sort of prank."

31

Coach K was suspended and crew practice was canceled for winter break. He flew home to Russia and left Vaughn the keys to the boathouse and even the keys to his Boston Whaler. Vaughn was

coughing violently and spitting up green gunk, and walking bare-
foot through the rocks and mud at the bottom of the river had
damaged the hardware in one of his knees so that, in addition to
his pneumonia, Vaughn needed new screws in one of his knees. I
felt sick, responsible — the guy who'd brought down Rich, Coach
K, and even Vaughn Warnicke — but Vaughn assured me that he
got these tune-ups all the time. "So that was fun," he said, and
punched me on the arm. "Got big plans for Christmas break?"

"Win the Scrabble tournament."

"So you're staying here?" he said.

"Depends — I'd need permission."

"And a place to stay," he said. "Well, please keep the guys in
line while I'm in California."

I assumed he meant to call Bob Peterbilt, who got depressed
on holidays and even on long weekends, and to make sure that
Jimmy Weems didn't spend the whole three weeks in Leah. Then
I found Coach K's keys in my bag of Scrabble tiles. Vaughn put
them in on a Friday, knowing I spent Saturdays playing against
myself. And I got this text from Coach K in Russia:

winston crwth you perform beautiful gesture

Vaughn, by "keep in line," meant that I would be coaching the
crew team over winter break. But we weren't allowed to practice
and they would all be far away — except Mike and Pat Siptroth,
twin brothers from Wilkes-Barre whose father was a priest and
whose birth had never been satisfactorily explained given Father
Siptroth's vow of celibacy — and I didn't know how I was supposed
to coach the team from my father's house. I had no idea what was
in the jar of water that I'd shown to Dr. Weir and still didn't really
understand how frackwater could be making Hale kids sick. But
things must be bad for Dr. Weir to offer to drive me to Harrisburg.

32

Fitler Hall was being dug up from the inside out — the old pipes, sinks, and toilets being torn out by their roots — and the noise was deafening, so we held the last meeting of Scrabble club before winter break in the cafeteria. Mr. U seemed to fall asleep with his head on his elbows on his tray, Alfredo sauce flecking a few of his gray hairs white. I felt sorry for him and couldn't stop staring; Thomasina seemed mortally embarrassed and held up her hands like blinders around her eyes.

I shook Mr. U's shoulder and put his things in his bag for him. "Come on," I said, "we're going to play somewhere with a little more privacy."

"Do I look that bad?" he said.

"You look doubleplusungood."

Mr. U sipped tea and did better in Dr. Weir's library. "Scrab?" we said occasionally, but he would ignore us, or pretend not to hear, and once or twice dropped his pen and fell asleep. I was sure his notes were for his masterpiece — the beast that kept him up at night and made him look so haunted, sick. I began to worry for our teacher's sanity after he dropped his notebook and I picked it up for him and saw that, instead of beautiful verses about love or fleeting youth, or even a poem about the opening of a bridge or the first day of spring, Mr. U seemed to be copying the words in our Scrabble games. Rich said his dad "didn't write," and I now saw what Rich meant. Mr. U had published poems that he found etched in metal at rest stops, or spelled out by marching bands at high school football games, or scrawled in the margins of an Amish guide to animal husbandry, and in this way he really was the poet of Pennsylvania.

He loved all books and seemed particularly interested in the books he couldn't reach in Dr. Weir's library — the *Tonalite-Vesuvius* volume of the eleventh edition of *Encyclopedia Britan-*

nica — or couldn't find in the Hale library. Although the funny thing was that he got a blank, faraway look when you told him these same books were available for pennies on the Internet. Tonight he got Hose to stand on a chair to try for *Tonalite–Vesuvius* and poor Hose promptly cut his hand on a nail.

"Another reading injury," Mr. U said. Hose was bleeding and all three of us stood waiting for Mr. U to list more reading injuries. Excessive reading would explain his pale skin and bloodshot eyes, but not his bad breath or the oily smell on his clothes. And it might explain why he looked up at Dr. Weir's blank diploma and seemed to lose his train of thought.

Hose hauled himself off to the infirmary and Mr. U sat down with a book of photographs. He found an even bigger book and laid it across his legs, and I watched these two books flatten him until he actually fell asleep. Thomasina's parents were somewhere in the house but this was close, very close, to being alone with her.

"So what are you doing for winter break?" I whispered.

"Depends," Thomasina said.

"On what?"

"I need to get my driver's license so we can go to Harrisburg."

"You and me?"

"Yes, dummy, so we can play in the Scrabble tournament."

"Mr. U can't drive?" I said.

Thomasina shuddered and I got the idea that she'd driven in his car and that the two of them had been in an accident. But she was shuddering because I'd forced her to repeat something Mr. U said to her. "Real writers don't drive."

"That is idiotic."

"Yes. Also real writers don't do their own laundry, or their own dishes, or fill out their own paperwork for their Dark Scholarships."

"Thomasina?"

"What?" she said.

"Tell me what you see in him."

"I feel sorry for him."

"Oh?"

"Because he is in love with me."

"As opposed to Rich who just wanted to have sex with you? Do you know how much time he spent on your stupid guessing game?"

"My stupid . . . ?" she said, as if trying to remember one of several games she played with the Urlachers.

"Scrabble winter rules," I said, "where Rich says you 'do' the verbs."

"But not sex."

"But other things?" I said.

"I play Rich that way because the poor guy can barely read and has potato moments every day."

"Rich has what?" Kenneth Duong had laughed and called my incredible, record-shattering performance on Ratty Duty — breaking thirty-five glasses because I dropped the freaking rack — a "potato moment" too.

"A lot of moments when people see how dumb he is."

"But why —" Mr. U stirred and smacked his lips and I let my question drop. One thing all three of my high schools had in common was that most girls — in this case the girl — seemed to go for assholes. Rich wrote about his trips to the Contraceptive Variety Store and had a huge following. I said things like "granites for ingrates" and played Scrabble against myself — making me more of a dweeb — until I wrote my poem and became the next Kid Who Might Kill Himself.

Thomasina had a point. Reckless as Rich's behavior had been, he'd become a reporter and had spent a lot of time reading stiff Victorian and gory medieval love poetry, searching for new words for "sex." And I often found him playing Scrabble against JANE in the library. "So you let Rich think that you might actually go to bed with him. But all that really happened was Rich reading books."

"And he got suspended."

"What about you and Mr. U? Are you two —"

"Not here," she said. Thomasina rose and straightened her thick wool skirt. The words "not here" thrilled me and suggested that we were going on a long walk in the woods, or a short walk to her room. But she dropped the bag of Scrabble tiles with a clack and woke up Mr. U.

"Mm," he said. "What time is it?"

"Almost sign-in," Thomasina said. "So almost time for Win to go. Where is that potato book?"

"It's not under U?" he said.

"No."

"Well, then, check under P."

Thomasina climbed the three remaining steps on the ladder and put one foot on the broken nub of the fourth and seemed like she was going to clamber up the shelves.

"Here," I said, and climbed up next to her. Her hair smelled like lavender and the nape of her neck smelled like pepper, wine, and raspberries. "Swoon" was the kind of word for which Mr. U flunked a poem, calling it a cliché, but swooning next to Thomasina on a ladder in her library felt like the closest I might come at Hale to losing my virginity.

Of course it's hard to separate the thrill of standing next to her from the thrill and horror of what happened next. She pointed to *The Potato Moment*, a book with a dusty brown cover that I pulled down in such a way that it flopped open to this point where the binding had been cracked: "To T., with great affection, from your follower U." The pretty handwriting bordered on calligraphy and suggested a side of Mr. U that only she had seen.

"What the hell?"

"It's about a guy who misspells 'potato.'"

"No," I hissed, "what the hell is with this inscription?"

"Unrequited love," she said.

33

I took *The Potato Moment* home. It was worse than publishing his son's letters as poetry and seemed to be about Rich if Rich were the vice president. Unlike Mr. U's other books, it was more of a novel or a prose poem, except the protagonist's voice was so beautifully, perfectly, transcendently *stupid* that I guessed Mr. U had "found" these words the way he found poems in old newspapers.

Among the many lines that reminded me of Rich:

What a waste it is to lose
One's Mind. Or not to have
A mind is being very wasteful.
How true that is.

But for all his mistakes, the vice president's life and his career don't come truly unglued until he spells "potato" p-o-t-a-t-o-e at a junior high school spelling bee.

34

In the end, I simply crammed the bruised apples, pears, chocolate chip cookies, and a few stale rolls from the last meal in the dining hall into my backpack and hauled them to my room, locked the door, sat down, and waited for the rest of the Hale School to go home. Everyone in Fitler closed his windows for the break, turning the second floor into an oven and baking me while I slept, so that I got a nosebleed and had a nightmare that I was drinking a bag of blood in the Hannah Penn cafeteria.

I woke up choking with the blood streaming down my face. Hannah Penn had been so hot and dry that we walked around with tissues crammed in our nostrils as if we'd all been in fights — and the school, after I left, only bought a new boiler after these two Goth girls began to walk around with the blood streaming down their necks and staining their shirts until they looked like they'd been stabbed. Washing my face would mean walking to the bathroom — and Dr. and Mrs. Goltz would hear my steps, if not the water in the pipes — so I stripped to my underwear and tried to go back to sleep.

"Is he dead?" a woman said.

I sat up. I'd slept all night and kicked the blankets around so that Mrs. Goltz could see the dried blood on my chest and could very nearly see my erection.

"What are you doing here?" she said. Dr. Goltz stood behind her with a bucket and a mop. The white circles around his eyes suggested he'd been pulled away from a session at his microscope.

"I'm sorry — I overslept."

"Get out of our house," she said.

"Can I take a shower?"

"In the river, for all I care."

Such was my thanks for letting them know their water was flammable. Mrs. Goltz had the wrinkled, thick, elephantine ankles of a Scrabbler, and I worried she would hear the jingling of Coach K's keys as I grabbed my bag of tiles, or wonder why I had not grabbed the board or my dictionary. "I'll go call my dad," I said.

I had never seen Hale without people, and the dirty brick buildings made it look like a mill that had gone out of business. Loki the black dog was sitting as always by Dr. Weir's hitching post, curled up against the cold, and I wanted to give him some food but didn't think he'd like fruit and dogs can't eat chocolate.

Vaughn gave me three keys in all — for the front door to Dreissegacker, for Coach K's Boston Whaler, and for the door to his office. Vaughn could barely be bothered with fracking or the Feldkircher kid — even after he shot him — and my only thought on seeing the cot, the space heater, and the mini fridge in Coach K's office was that Vaughn must really want me to win the tournament, or win Thomasina.

I put my jar of frackwater in the fridge and turned on Coach K's computer and had blindly typed out most of an email to my mother before noticing the characters were Cyrillic. I was supposed to fly to California for winter break and had been trying to explain that I would be staying here. My mother's email was always being hacked, and my father and I were always receiving emails in her name in French, in Japanese, in numerical code as if she'd been hacked by a computer operating on its own. Russian gibberish would be no less successful than some of my other attempts to tell her about my life — and might even interest her if she thought that I'd been hacked — except that I could see Coach K's computer *correcting* what I wrote, so that it wasn't gibberish, or may not have been gibberish, and my cover would be blown if she took the whole thing for an email from Coach K and she tried to write him back.

Getting dressed in front of the Goltzes had been so stressful — they didn't watch but neither did they turn away from the nearly naked kid hopping into his pants — that I had forgotten the charger for my phone and only had enough juice for this quick call with my dad.

"It's me. Can you tell Mom I won't be coming to California?"

"She'll be dis —"

"I'm staying here and I don't exactly have permission."

"How will you —"

"I've got a place to sleep. I just need —"

"Valley Forge," he said. "Washington's army nearly starved to death because Congress couldn't be bothered to feed them. The farms around Valley Forge had already been picked clean and sutlers wouldn't sell them food because their early, American money was worthless, so they lived on a diet of fire cakes . . ."

My phone was about to die and I would have had enough time to tell him where to send food except these last two words piqued my curiosity. "Fire cakes?"

"A simple mixture of flour and water from the Schuylkill, which Washington's men fried —"

35

Coach K's keyboard had English characters, too, but I couldn't figure out how to switch from the Cyrillic and could only "write" to people in English by copying words from his other documents, or copying individual letters when I couldn't find words that were appropriate — a ridiculous system that was as arduous, as painstaking, as printing a message with movable type. I longed to communicate with my father, with Thomasina, and got desperately lonely within an hour of sitting on Coach K's cot. But what I "wrote" came out sounding so stilted, so mechanical — impossible to find the right words on his computer — that my pain didn't sound real and I wondered if this was how Rich felt while trying to express himself.

I told my father to send food and spent two days eating cookies, pears, and playing computer games with the brightness turned way down. Hearing more about Valley Forge would have been helpful as I made the great mistake of rejecting the bruised apples on my first day, after which they got so soft and sunken that I simply threw them out. Today was December 22 and the tournament was on January 2, and I calculated that I needed twenty to thirty meals and at least one or two good books to survive winter break in the boathouse. Coach K had an old wall calendar of Leningrad and a girl-a-day calendar hidden behind some pens and PowerBars in his desk. The girls wore furs, bikinis, and military uniforms, and some of them had websites whose Cyrillic characters I could have pecked out except, in the same way that I'd never had a wet dream because I was too afraid the dream-girl would get pregnant, I was terrified of getting a virus.

I sat listening for the growl of the UPS truck and watched through binoculars as it drove up to Fitler and as Dr. Goltz signed for my father's care package. I knew it was from my father because the green logo for his favorite kind of beer appeared on the box. The truck came back the next day and this package, a bag or sack that had been wrapped in tape, must have been from my mother. I emailed them both and told them to stop sending food, and found that writing was getting easier as I built up a store of words and whole phrases that I could simply cut and paste. Building "love" out of *l* and *o* and *v* and *e* had seemed like a waste of time because I rarely told my parents that I loved them. But once I did and had "love" all ready to go, it was like I was in love with everyone. I wrote to Mr. U and told him how much I would love to take Orwell 101. I wrote to Thomasina and told her how much I'd love to get together over the holidays. I wrote to Rich and left comments on his articles for the *Derrick* and must have written something to give myself away because I woke up Christmas morning to see footprints in the snow. I stuck my head outside and saw a plastic bag that bulged at the bottom, suggesting an orange or a muffin, and pulled it inside and found a thick black piece of shale. It looked like the piece that had been stolen from Dr. Goltz's classroom and must have been a gift from Rich. I dumped "Thanks a lot," "I love it," "I hope you're having a great winter break," and some of my other prefabricated phrases in the box underneath one of Rich's articles.

"Dude," he wrote, "what's wrong with you?"

"What do you mean what's wrong with me?"

"I mean you sound so normal."

I took a lot of midmorning naps and added an afternoon nap and was thrilled to wake up in the dark, thinking I could cross off another day in Leningrad, except that it was barely 3:30 and I was just in a shadow cast by one of the Endless Mountains — a finger of darkness that blotted out the boathouse and now crept toward the Wodtke-Weirs'. My stomach hurt and bile was rising in my throat. The stone floor felt like ice and my whole body was stooped like my father's after he accidentally fell asleep on the couch. I picked up the piece of shale and used it to draw a game of hangman on the floor, trying to figure out how I could play against myself. I broke it in half to make a better nib and was holding both halves under my nose when I felt a strange tingling in my spine and a buzzing in my brain and realized the shale was *making me high*. A faint and fleeting sense of euphoria — a high like trying to fill your stomach with the smell of food — during which I decided that I'd done the right thing by staying here and that the Hale School needed me.

I left the plastic bag outside that night with a note that said, "Rich, or anyone — I could really use some food." The bag and the note were still there in the morning, and so were the old footprints in the snow. I followed them through the woods and paused at the Feldkirchers' NO TRESPASSING sign — then walked on with their jar of water held out in front of me. I knocked on their door and the kid answered and said, "Did you give it to LaRue?"

"Not yet. Next week. Do you have any food?"

The kid brought me what looked like a six-pack of beer but

was in fact six more samples of tap water in fat test tubes, each of which had been labeled with SUITE CODE 818 and a little shield that showed a ship, a plow, some wheat — the seal of Pennsylvania.

"I can't give her this," I said. "It's a meeting in her office in Harrisburg, probably with reporters and TV cameras."

"But you'll get these tested?"

"Kid," I said, "these things say they've been tested already. They all say, 'Does not contain significant amount of calcium, iron, potassium —'"

"Yeah, well, these tests can't be right. My dad asked them to test it for radioactivity and it's like they tested it for vitamins."

"Eight-eighteen."

"What is that?" he said.

I believed fiercely that this number was a lie — as a Scrabble score, if nothing else — but the number seemed to mean nothing to the kid. "I don't know what it is," I said. "But I've still got your other jar and I'll give it to LaRue."

The kid would not let me into the house and it was a sign, per-haps, that I'd learned something during my cold, lonely week in the boathouse that I was happy to stand there with the wind bit-ing my cheeks and the porch creaking under my feet and a squirrel chittering. The kid cursed loudly, and I worried there was some new problem with their water that I would be asked to solve. He came back with a milk crate full of bread, cereal, peanut but-ter, jelly, cookies, canned pineapple rings and canned pineapple chunks, and a plastic bag of rock candy on a stick — all covered with salsa, in which some of the glistening, little bits turned out to be broken glass. "I tripped."

"Is this all —"

"It's all we have. Although I know a place that will give you five bucks for that milk crate in Wyomingville."

The phone rang and the kid wrote down the name of the

place — a dairy farm — and then shooed me off the porch while talking on the phone. "Yes, sir. I'll get right on that, sir. Merry Christmas to you, too, sir."

I stuck around and wanted to ask how, exactly, a crate from a fracked dairy farm could be worth five bucks, but the kid shook his head and shot an imaginary gun at me. I walked back to the boathouse and was so hungry that I ate most of a jar of peanut butter with my fingers — chewing carefully in case I got a piece of glass. The salsa froze, and scraping this red muck with its chunks of peppers, glass, and onions off the rest of the food was such a bad job that I dumped it all in a plastic garbage bag and set out on the long walk to Wyomingville.

I walked down the hill from Hale to the highway and could not decide which was more dangerous — walking toward the tanker trucks bringing in all the water used to flush the gas out of the ground and getting sand and grit in my eyes, or walking with my back to them. Eventually, I sat on my crate and stuck out my thumb and counted sixty-three trucks before heading back up the hill. I couldn't remember if hitchhiking was illegal in Pennsylvania and decided it should be after I accidentally looked a trucker in the eyes — eyes like a mean, hungry dog. The trucks ran twenty-four hours a day, and I'd heard Dr. Goltz say that it would be forty or fifty years before the state was completely fracked and that meant . . .

A car was coming down the hill and I ran into the woods. Driving slowly, firmly, with a blank look on her face was Thomasina. She had promised me a ride to Harrisburg if she got her license and my heart fluttered at the sight.

Sitting in the front seat was Mr. U, her driving coach, gritting his teeth and bracing himself as if the car was going off a cliff.

Part Three

36

There are just a few really famous Scrabble games in history, most involving cheating, or failing to challenge a word that is not a word, or some other form of humiliation. And with Thomasina sitting sullenly across from me, then sitting in the audience of the Pennsylvania State Scrabble Championship, I would play in two of them.

Thomasina drove us to Harrisburg in the rain and kept waking Mr. Urlacher up because she only had her learner's permit and needed to have an adult in the car at all times, and thought he wouldn't count as one unless he was awake. He made her stop for coffee and then spat it out and made her drive back so he could get espresso. He had a splitting headache and would not play Ghost with us — a word game that is like the opposite of Scrabble in that you try to keep adding letters without making a word — and would not let us listen to the radio. Neither of them asked what I'd done over winter break, except to say that I looked thin. While I hoped this was because they each knew where I'd been the whole time, and didn't necessarily want the other one to know, I think the real reason was that they just didn't care.

Mr. U squirmed in boredom when she drove the speed limit and braced himself in fear when she drove over it. He winced at the sight of the state capitol — a sprawling, stone, Kafkaesque complex with a sickly green dome in the middle — but seemed to perk up as we got closer and the streets got more and more crowded with cars and people, many of them carrying tarps and tents and plastic jugs as if they were on a camping trip.

"Help," Thomasina said. "Where the hell do I park?"

"Here," he said, and handed her a blue-and-yellow sign that said PENNSYLVANIA STATE OFFICIAL. "Put that in the window and we can park anywhere."

"You're a state official?"

"Yes. Trevonia Dark says these things are magic. Make your car invisible. Good for speeding, drunk driving, you name it, but let's not push our luck."

"Trevonia will be here?" I said.

"As a coach. I'm told her son is the real Scrabbler."

"Two more people trying to get a meeting with LaRue?" I said.

"David Dark is a lobbyist for Dark Oil and Gas and the son of their CEO. Trevonia is the founder and the biggest funder of Dark Scholarships. So LaRue, if anything, will be skulking after them."

"You mean stalking."

"What?" he said.

"You mean stalking LaRue." Unlike Mr. U to make this kind of mistake — and another sign that there was something wrong with him. Thomasina threw Mr. U's "magic" sign on the floor and turned the car around as if he had made such promises before. She got back on the highway and drove to the other side of the capitol, but it was the same story here — except the cars were mostly old or rusty and many had bumper stickers with the clean blue flame of Dark Oil & Gas.

He popped the top off a bottle of Advil and shook pills into his mouth. I thought Mr. U was sick from writing. Thomasina thought he was sick from unrequited love. The truth was simpler and had been staring me in the face.

"Taking coral pills?" I said.

"What?" he said.

"I see you're taking several coral-colored pills."

"I don't know how they do it."

"Who?"

"People who work two jobs," he said. "Maybe if I was younger, but my back is killing me. They give me a Dark Scholarship and the Darks give me one of the first leases in this part of the state, but how do they expect me to write when I'm sick? And how would they like it if I woke up one day and decided to tell the truth?"

"Fracking made you sick?" I said.

"Dark said they'd take care of me, and I got two hundred bucks an acre — twice what my neighbors got. But it's like the gold rush and the first leases are the worst. Today those same leases go for two thousand bucks an acre."

"But your cough —"

"Partially my fault," he said. "I got my water switched but kept drinking the beer I'd brewed with well water. Also, there's this group that actually drinks the frackwater to show how bad it is, and I wanted to help them so I drank a little bit."

"A bit?"

"A glass."

"You drank a glass of fracking chemicals?"

"Remember those English poets who drank their own urine? Van Gogh who drank absinthe —"

"Piss is clean," Thomasina said disgustedly. "And van Gogh had xanthopsia. Win, that means he saw the world as if through yellow sunglasses."

She knew I'd never know this word, and I loved that about her. "Let me get this straight," I said. "You're mad at Dark because the wells on your property haven't made you rich, or as rich as your neighbors. But you're sick because you drank a glass —"

"Other people drank glasses of the water from their wells."

"In protest?"

"In their beer, their lemonade, in their concentrated juice. Some got sick and went to the hospital, and it turns out there's a law that doctors aren't allowed to tell people if they're being poisoned by these chemicals."

"Doctors aren't allowed to tell people *which* chemicals," Thomasina said, and grabbed my leg. Thomasina's hand was hot and surprisingly strong, and this gave me wild ideas because bookworms are famous for their cold, clammy hands. I could not imagine being the only guy at a school for girls, and now saw how I might have panicked and fallen under the spell of someone much older — anything to have a friend and a kind of buffer against all those girls.

"Exactly," he said, taking credit for being right when, in fact, Thomasina had corrected him. "So my friends, these *roqueros*, diagnosed themselves by drinking diesel, butane, arsenic, and all these other chemicals and seeing if their symptoms were similar to people who drank water from their wells —"

"What's *roqueros*? Rocks?" I said.

"SoFoPo one-oh-one," he said. "The *roqueros* were a group of Cuban activists who weren't allowed to listen to heavy metal rock, who were actually imprisoned for listening to rock, so they gave themselves AIDS."

"Wow," I said.

"My problem is that people got sick drinking their tap water and Dark ignored them. Then people got really sick drinking fracking chemicals and Dark exposed the fact that many of them were the same people who chained themselves to the Ben Franklin Bridge to protest the use of gas-powered cars. I drank the wastewater that comes out of the wells — the stuff they use to deice the roads — and it's full of heavy metals that are supposed to be a mile underground. And it's radioactive."

"So?" I said. "In Rocks for Jocks we learned that bananas are radioactive."

Mr. U's behavior was arguably heroic, or at least foolish *and* heroic, but something about his story turned us against him. I liked the idea of him striking it rich, and was very grateful for my own Dark Scholarship. And I sort of loved the idea of exposing the truth about fracking by the simple act of drinking a glass of water. But the maddening thing about Mr. U was that he wanted to strike it rich *and* still tell the shocking truth. He complained about LaRue and having to write about coal, the Johnstown Flood, Three Mile Island, and our state's seemingly endless series of natural and man-made disasters, but Mr. U loved being the poet laureate. In his mind, he was a sick, miserable failure, a man who'd poisoned himself. But he still expected the rest of us to see him as Sir Walter Raleigh and still wanted to be him — the man who failed to find El Dorado but got rich writing about his failure.

37

Thomasina drove around the city for a long time, refusing to believe that Mr. U's sign would make her car invisible. Eventually, she parked in a lot for employees of the Pennsylvania Department of Revenue — the state poet parking with its tax collectors — and got out and knelt as if she was going to be sick. Thomasina's lovely lips could make her look sensuous even when she sat slumped with a bowl of oatmeal. Her clear gray eyes could make her seem wise even when she had no idea what was going on. I now saw that her laughter and jokes at Mr. U's expense had been hiding her shame and embarrassment. She may have turned against Mr. U long ago, the moment she stepped into his house and he became just a middle-aged man with a Scrabble set, a water buffalo, and frothy yellow vats of beer. But she only showed it now.

Thomasina took my hand and Mr. U walked several steps behind us. "You!" yelled a man waving a flag with a rattlesnake and the words DON'T TREAD ON ME. "Hey, yeah, you, yeah, Urlacher!" Our hands clenched in horror and for the same reason — the fear that Mr. U had just found a poem on the streets of Harrisburg and that we would be in it. We were walking along one side of the capitol and through a crowd of several hundred people, many of them holding signs for or against fracking. There were more signs against but they were uglier — dirty, soggy, stained and smeared as if with fracking chemicals — and I found it easier to look at the clean blue flame of Dark Oil & Gas.

"Urlacher!" yelled an old woman with a gut and her gray hair tied back in a ponytail. "Hey, U, that's right, I'm talking to you! Get your ass over here."

The old woman seemed to belong to a motorcycle gang, and many of them poked and punched Mr. U on the arm. He blushed and bowed his head as if their love would take the form of physical abuse. It was all too easy to imagine how Mr. U, who was both the bard of the oil and gas industry and a hero to his *roqueros*, was a hero to these people, too.

"Is this the kid?" the old woman said. I was about to make

a jerk of myself by saying yes and slapping Mr. Urlacher on the back, as if he were the kid, when I looked into her face and saw something familiar. She wore steel-toed boots and a T-shirt with flames but had the soft face, the gut, and the squinting, kindly eyes of Benjamin Franklin. "Does he know what to do when he meets LaRue?" she said.

"He'll know what to do," said Mr. U.

"When do we meet LaRue?" Thomasina said, as if this part of the plan was new to her.

"We meet her after Winston wins the Scrabble tournament. LaRue loves to get her picture taken with the champion."

"Is this because she won't meet with you herself?" Thomasina challenged him.

Mr. U's face turned a milky shade of pink and he shrugged as if we now knew his secret. All fall I thought my future depended on getting Mr. U to like me and to be my Scrabble coach, giving me the chance to play in this tournament. But Mr. U must have been playing hard to get because he was just as desperate to have me win so he could get a meeting with the governor.

"And is this the girl?" the old woman said, pointing to Thomasina.

"The girl?" Thomasina said, and turned on Mr. U. "What did you tell these people about me?"

"Easy," he said, and tried to touch her arm. "I just said I'd be here with two kids, two chances for us to see the governor."

Thomasina tightened her grip on my hand and we left Mr. U smoking a cigar and sipping amber-colored stuff from a white plastic jug. "Oh, my God," Thomasina said. "I am such an idiot. I should have known a man so in love with the sound of his own voice would tell people that I came to his house."

"I don't care —" I began to say.

"Little girl," Thomasina said, touching the hand of a girl drinking from a cloudy plastic jug. "Did your parents say that water is okay to drink?" The girl nodded. "Are you sure? Because there are a lot of people here with water that is really bad to drink." The girl frowned and tugged at something sticking out of her damp, ratty coat — a stick that spread its wings and turned out to be a feather.

"Did you bring that water from your house, or did you buy it in a store?"

"The jug is from our house," she said.

"And what about the water?"

"By waiting in that line," she said, pointing to a line of people, all with soda bottles, or white plastic jugs, or jerry cans as if the water here could be used to start a car. Some sat on the ground and some were in wheelchairs, and the ones standing at the bottom of a slick, gray mossy wall looked like serfs come to collect bread crusts. Or so I thought from far away. Thomasina and I walked toward the front of this line and now saw that many of these shivering, wretched-looking folks wore suits and ties and many wore the Orwellian — numbers but no names on the back — football jerseys of the Nittany Lions, and a few of the kids wore jeans and shirts that were ripped or stained as if with acid — a look that was popular among the kids at Clovis Friends.

A girl was stunningly beautiful, with red hair, a turned-up nose, and pale white ears that poked through her hair. And she was so bored looking that I dared to talk to her. "Where does this line go?" I said.

"The line to see LaRue," she said. "Or that's what I used to think. Now I hear it's the line to get free water from LaRue's bathroom. Which is still pretty cool."

"How long have you been doing this?"

"Since Dark Oil and Gas uglified my school."

She grunted "uglified" and my mouth got hot and dry. Rich had warned me that the way to get a beautiful girl to talk to you was not to look at her—that being beautiful could make a girl crazy and that the cure was for you to ignore her. This girl had a pale pink scar under her chin, and something about the whiteness of her face made it stand out ostentatiously. The pink as shocking as blood against her alabaster skin. I had meant "how long have you been standing in this line," but, beautiful or not, she was the second girl I had talked to since September and I was more than happy to mean what she thought I meant. "They are drilling at your school?"

"No, my school's in Pittsburgh where fracking is illegal. I mean they've given so much money to the school that everything is the Dark Wing or Dark Hall or the Dark Observatory."

"I'm a Dark Scholar."

"Where?"

"The Hale School for Boys."

"What's your name?"

"Winston Crwth."

"So are you girl-crazy?"

"Yes," I said so quickly that we said "y" at the same time and I just added "es." An older girl at Hannah Penn had asked me if I was girl-crazy and I'd hemmed and hawed before saying yes—a response that made me seem ashamed of liking girls.

"There's a cure."

"They already put saltpeter in the lemonade."

"Ha," she said. "I mean a better cure than that."

"Have a girlfriend?"

"Yes," she said.

"So how long have you been standing in this line?"

"Since this morning. Though it's like I've been *waiting* to stand in this line since the Aliquippa Incident."

"The what?" I said.

"You know how they have nowhere to put all the wastewater that comes out of the wells?" she said.

"I thought they just dumped it in rivers and used it to deice the roads."

"Right," she said. "But in Aliquippa they sent it to the plant where they treat shit — the actual plant where they make shit and piss drinkable — and it rotted out their shit-eating machinery."

"So where do they send it now?"

"Ohio. Want to wait in line with me? Or will that scare your girlfriend off?"

"She is not my girlfriend."

"Is she his?"

I turned around and saw that Thomasina had gone back to Mr. U. She was holding two empty milk jugs, wielding them like boxing gloves. She jabbed at Mr. U to get his attention and then jabbed in my general direction. He looked drunk but was sick and may also have been in love. Then she gave him a jug and pointed at me with her finger. Like a dog, he stared at it, the point of pointing beyond him.

"Get in line!" I yelled at him. "It's the line to see LaRue!"

"Too long!" he said.

"But that's the point!"

"No," the girl with the red hair said to me, "the point is that waiting in this line is easier than waiting for clean water where we live."

I liked this girl and liked the idea of this protest, but hated the reality — waiting in the cold all night, without coffee, food, or a warm place to sit.

"Who's that man? He's cute," she said. "He looks kind of familiar."

"He's the PA poet laureate."

"What's his name?"

"Thomas Urlacher."

"Oh, my God, I love 'Love'!" she said, and I had to laugh because there was something about Mr. U and his simple poetry that made people happy. "Why don't you guys stand with me? I know people with a tent. Come on—you never know," she said. "In case we have to wait all night."

I looked up at the capitol and felt sick to my stomach. The line seemed to be moving but I saw this was because it was getting *wider*, not because people were getting in to see LaRue. "You're kidding."

"No," she said. "Some of the people who got all the way to LaRue's bathroom came back and said it took them days."

"I'll be back."

"After what?" she said.

"I win a Scrabble tournament."

38

Among its many mistakes—like giving me a scholarship—I bet Dark Oil & Gas wished they had called horizontal high-pressure hydraulic fracturing something besides "fracking." Kids said it like a curse and the jocks in Rocks for Jocks would ask Goltz about fracking just to hear him say it, too. I drew an F and a blank and had a strange, self-destructive urge to FRACK on my first turn of my first game in the tournament—knowing full well that it was not a word in Scrabble—except that I was playing a ten-year-old girl and FRACK seemed a little rude.

The girl was not so delicate and jumped out to an early lead by playing HAOLE. A Hawaiian slur for people not from Hawaii. I played dirty words all the time but tried to draw the line at slurs—tried and failed, as I only beat this girl by playing HAOLES.

The tournament was in a ballroom with fifteen rows of fifteen boards — a board for each square in the board — and I could see the table where Thomasina was supposed to be only by standing up, and standing was against the rules. I had walked here alone and she had not followed me. Also against the rules was talking, wearing headphones, using a computer or other handheld device, and signaling of any kind, although this last ban was hard to enforce because some of the younger players waved to their parents in the audience or actually jumped for joy after beating this or that old troglodyte, and many of the adults twitched or jerked their hands uncontrollably.

I beat a man so fat he hid his chair and seemed to float above the board. I beat a man whose knees knocked against the table and whose bony, pimply legs brought to mind chicken flesh. I fell behind Barbara, a woman who kept swatting at her ear, and who grunted, cursed, and made strange noises under her breath. Scrabblers are a baggy, sedentary lot, and while I didn't mind the thought of sacrificing my body for the game — the long hours squinting and sitting on my bed — I hated the idea that I would lose my mind.

"Aa ab ad ae ag ah . . ." Barbara sounded like she was gargling. I was wrong. She didn't have Tourette's but was reciting the list of two-letter words — chanting them as if possessed and speaking in tongues. Barbara sang every one, from "aa" all the way to "yo," then took a deep breath and began to sing the three's, "Aah aal aas aba abo abs aby . . ." She stopped when she got to "brr" and played this word on the board.

" 'Brrr,' " I said, and put an R on the end of her BRR. "Brr" and "brrr" are different spellings of the thing you say when you are cold. Both are permissible and are the kind of thing that, when I played them against kids at any of my three high schools, made them groan or gawk at me like I was some kind of freak. Even my

mother's friends on her farm in Oakland — the ones who said " 'e"
instead of "he" or "she," and " 's" instead of "his" or "hers" — found
the fact that I could play Scrabble without vowels, or, worse, *speak*
without vowels, to be disturbing.

Barbara's babbling belied the fact that she was brilliant, and I
only won our game by dumb luck. I was far behind and stuck with
four ls when I drew the X. " 'Xu' and 'xi,' " I said, playing the X on
a triple-letter square.

"Nice game," Barbara said, and shook my hand warmly and
even looked me in the eyes. She pulled out her cell phone and
made baby noises to what seemed to be a baby — babbling appro-
priately — so that I could no longer tell if Scrabble made her bab-
ble, or if she played well because of her babbling.

I applied Rich's philosophy of beautiful girls to my Scrabble
opponents and tried not to look at them. Some of the old men
looked like me if I'd seen a ghost — their eyes stunned, their faces
bleached — and some of the women wore the cold, hard expression my mother wore when reading my report card, and several
of the children looked or sounded like they had stepped from the
pages of *Charlie and the Chocolate Factory*: a girl who chewed
gum and talked energetically while I was trying to think; a girl
who wore white stockings and shiny black shoes with buckles and
complained bitterly that EE was the plural for "eyes."

I did not look at my next opponent as she sat across from me.
She smelled like vanilla and a bit like pepper, and I wanted to look
but had drawn one of the worst starting hands I'd ever seen. Us
are good in case you get the Q, but two Us are deadly, so I got rid
of mine with ULU for six points. An ulu is a knife.

My opponent played ULU through my L, a knife through my
knife, and I looked up to see Thomasina. "Hi," I said.

"Trying to think," she said.

"I'm sorry, I didn't see —"

"Your girlfriend says hello," she said.

"The redhead?"

"Her name is Jill. Not that you would think to ask."

"She is not my girlfriend. Did you leave her with Mr. Urlacher?"

Thomasina grimaced and then smiled despite herself, as if thrilled by the awfulness of leaving Jill with Mr. U. "He's upstairs. He got us a room. He saw you win your last few games and thinks you'll win the tournament."

"He's been here? I didn't see —"

"What is wrong with you?" she snapped. "A girl actually talks to you and you just walk away. You don't even ask her name."

"I like you."

She shook her head. "Don't do that — I'm impossible."

"Who is D?"

"Oh, my God," she said. "So you're spying on me, too?"

"Just in Leah. Only once. I opened the Scrabble set and saw that you'd played this guy D."

"David Dark. A sweet man who says you taught him how to swim."

"A man in a wheelchair?"

"Yes."

And now I remembered him. "That's a lie. All we did was play Scrabble by the pool."

"At Hale?"

"At Clovis Friends," I said. Playing Scrabble by a pool with a man in a wheelchair had been memorable — he'd been strangely thrilled when I challenged ABLEBODIED and told him it was not a word — but I'd never known his name. "Oh, my God, I think I know why Dark gave me a scholarship."

"It's your turn."

"David liked me and —"

"Win, not while I'm Scrabbling."

"Huh," I said, and played this word, and Thomasina copied me, playing both blank tiles and making them both Hs — a suicidal move because the blanks are the two best tiles in the bag. The look on her face could also be described as blank, and I thought of Stephen Ha and had the bad feeling that our game was about to alter reality. I played SULUS for five points — a Melanesian skirt and a poor play but an attempt to climb out of her trap. Incredibly, Thomasina had two Ss, too, and proved just how impossible she could be by copying me a third time and creating this Gordian knot:

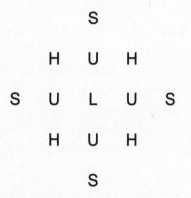

A board to which it is impossible to add a word. I was actually ahead by 46–19 at this point but didn't see how I could go. Tournament games are timed and you lose ten points a minute once your clock's gone negative. I went on to lose this game by 19–6, the lowest combined score in Scrabble history and one of its most humiliating defeats. And while I resigned before my score went negative — before I fell into Minusland — my clock's still running in my mind and my score is now less than minus eighteen million.

39

I can't take all the credit for destroying Linda King LaRue and didn't set out to do much more than play her in a Scrabble game. There were literally thousands of people waiting to see LaRue that weekend, or fill their jugs and jerry cans with water from her bathroom. But I was the only one with whom LaRue let down her guard.

The other extraordinary thing was that I had the courage to stand up to the Fracking King. I was never very good at challenging authority. I was the meek kid who might correct a bully's grammar before getting punched in the gut. The B student who had read his father's gluey copy of *The New Soviet Encyclopedia* and knew for a fact that America gave women the right to vote *after* the Soviets, but who said nothing because his history teacher was twenty-three and wore high heels and had a low, husky voice. Yet Scrabble made me fearless, almost violent, and while I could sit back and let Dark wreck the Skulking River or poison the wells in hundreds of homes in northeast Pennsylvania, I had to do something when LaRue offended my Scrabble sensibilities.

It's not that I got so far in the Scrabble tournament. It's the things I did to win. After beating me in the lowest-scoring game in history, Thomasina was accosted by tournament officials who wanted to make sure that our game was not a fake, a joke by two prep school kids, and by a TV reporter with lily-white teeth who asked, "What's your secret?" and seemed to think our game was scandalous. I felt sick to my stomach and felt a sharp ache in my wrist — a pain in a spot where I had been bitten by a dog. That had been idiotic, too. Never touch a dog's bowl while he is eating.

Despite my loss, I finished in the top thirty-two and won a spot in the finals tomorrow. I went up to our room and found Mr. U sleeping in one of the beds. "Our" may be too strong a word.

Thomasina said that Mr. U got us a room and I assumed "us" was us, but it could have been them. The TV was on and the bathroom light was on and Mr. U's toothpaste-smeared toiletry bag gaped at me, but I knew, from living alone with my dad since I was six, never to look in the bag of a middle-aged man.

Mr. U lay on his back and snored and looked sicker than ever, a book and the TV remote rising, falling on his chest.

"You backed the wrong horse," I said.

"Mmm," he said.

"Sorry if you don't get your meeting with the governor."

Mr. U smacked his lips and sounded like he was trying to talk with a sock stuck in his throat.

"What?"

"You're not a horse," he said. "And I'd never bet on Thomasina Wodtke-Weir. The girl plays Scrabble beautifully."

"But not to win."

"A fatal flaw," he said.

I went to turn the TV off and now saw the reporter with the lily-white teeth talking to David Dark. A blue blanket covering his chest and legs made him look like an old man, and it kept quivering as if David had a small animal in his lap.

"So, David," the reporter said, "what's the secret of your success?"

"Scrabble drives girls wild," he said, and grinned wolfishly.

I was tempted to run downstairs and ask David about 818 — his purported Scrabble score and the number written on my jar of frackwater. I might have to beat David to win the tournament, and this thought disturbed me, not least because his parents were paying my tuition. "Do you know this guy?" I asked Mr. U. "He's my competition."

"Sure," he said. "The trick to beating the Darks is to create a coalition of urban and suburban environmentalists who're terrified their water and the pH of their craft beer will get thrown off by fracking chemicals, and get them to work with the Amish and the Mennonites and the other poor souls who can taste the benzene in their potatoes."

"No," I said, "I mean I need to beat him at Scrabble."

"In New York they're fighting Dark with trust fund kids and Wall Street guys who summer in the Finger Lakes. They've got John Lennon's kid and a freaking fracking film. Here we've got the poet laureate, and I'm about to be replaced by the wife of the CEO of Dark Oil and Gas. Have you read Trevonia's poems? They read like cookie recipes."

"Get a grip, Mr. U," I said. "You're a high school English teacher in a hotel in Harrisburg. I am trying to beat David Dark in a game of Scrabble."

"Stall for time and hope the kid has to go to the bathroom."

"That's horrendous."

"Oh?" he said. "You don't think David will exploit your weaknesses?"

Mr. U pushed a button and the TV went on mute. He pushed another button and several rows of small, garish boxes appeared on the screen—some the color of blood and some the color of flesh. "So what should we watch?" he said.

I chose a movie near the upper right corner of the screen—a box just a few moves from the upper left—but Mr. U did something odd and moved the cursor down and around the screen, scurrying like a rat. He was trying to avoid movies for adults as if passing through these squares would get him in trouble. This was unlike Mr. U, a man who let us use dirty words so long as they fit a poem's meter and rhyme scheme.

He had closed his eyes and was breathing deeply when the door creaked open and Thomasina said, "I'm back."

"Shh," I said.

"What the hell?" she said. "Where am I supposed to sleep?"

"Here," Mr. U said. He sat up and put a few things in a bag and then bent over awkwardly as if the bag had dragged him down.

"Help him," Thomasina said.

I helped him by putting on my jacket and my shoes, cramming my copy of the Scrabble dictionary, fourth edition, in my pocket, and leaving him alone with Thomasina.

40

The way I beat David Dark is also despicable. I was walking through the hotel's revolving doors, clutching my coat to my chest and trying to decide between knocking on my grandfather's door or getting in the line to see LaRue—cutting in with Jill, if she would have me — when I saw David sitting in the bar, drinking his beer through a straw. David's blue blanket had fallen on the floor and I saw his right hand trembling in his lap.

"Sure hope you're left-handed," I said, picking up his blanket and putting it on his legs. A strange, insulting thing to say to some-one in a wheelchair . . . and yet I had the feeling that he'd be grate-ful if I made fun of him the way I would any other guy.

"No such luck," David said. "I am right-handed."

"I —"

"How's it feel to get the lowest score in Scrabble history? To be the guy who opened a black hole in the Scrabble universe?"

"That was unintentional."

"So what's it like?" David said, as if continuing some con-versation we'd had by the pool at Clovis Friends. I remembered beating him and remembered that he'd been too embarrassed to

swim because someone — his mother or his girlfriend — had accidentally signed him up for a class in which most of the swimmers
were little kids in swim diapers.

"What's Hale like? I used to think that Hale would be Hell, but
ever since they put an air conditioner in my room —"

"No — what's high school like?" he said.

David had thin, wooden legs. He had his mother's stiff shoulders, and while he was clearly smart, and clearly brilliant at Scrabble, I guessed that he'd been unable to attend school physically.

"Hard to say. I've been to three. They're all pretty different."

"Want a beer?"

"I'm seventeen."

"I am irresistible."

I drank a beer with David and learned that he had muscular
dystrophy. He could have been twenty or thirty or thirty-five. It
was hard to tell because his hands were soft as a child's, while his
face was haggard.

"Ablebodied."

I said this and a man drinking near us shot me a dirty look and
rose slightly in his seat — a dark, fatherly look as if I was bullying
David in his wheelchair.

David smiled. "That's very good," he said. "I told you I had a
word — the best word I'd ever seen, but you made me take it back.
Do you know how many times in my life I've been humiliated like
that?"

"I don't know. All the time?" I said.

"No, never," David said. "Ablebodied's not a word. Able-
hyphen-bodied is."

"You didn't like the hyphen because it's ugly, awkward, right?
A word that looks . . . what did you say?"

"I forget. The most boring thing about being in a wheelchair is
that people never challenge you."

"That seems wrong."

"It's terrible."

"No, I mean I disagree with your analysis. Don't we do it all the time?"

"In the wrong ways."

"Oh," I said.

"I told my mother about you and I even showed her some of the words you played, and she thought you had a real artistic sensibility."

"So you're —"

"Your guardian angel. You were nice to the cripple who —"

"I was mean."

"That's true," he said. "I still don't know how to swim." I couldn't tell if David's strange affinity for me meant that he wanted me to fight him all the time — a sparring partner who did not pull his punches — or because he thought I was actually good at heart and that he had saved me with a Dark Scholarship. "Do you know what I hate most about these tournaments?" he said.

"The cheats?"

David frowned. He'd leaned forward and touched my arm while saying, "cripple," as if sharing a secret, and I got the distinct feeling that he wanted me to say it, too — that saying it would make us friends. Hannah Penn was the kind of school where slurs could be a socially acceptable way of addressing another person — to show you weren't afraid of them — and I had been hazed, in part, because I wouldn't go along.

"Not enough girls," he said.

"I know one."

"A girl with gray hair who plays Scrabble sadistically? No, thank you. Not my type."

"No, another girl," I said. "A girl with red hair and lips like *sakura masu*."

David gawped. "What's that?" he said.

"Cherry salmon sushi in which the cherry is her tongue."

"Where is she?"

"In the line to see Linda King LaRue."

"I can help."

"You know her?"

"Yes. Dark money made her governor. Our family's been close to every governor since Penn."

"William or Hannah?"

"What?" he said.

"William died and left his wife to run the colony."

"So LaRue's not technically the first female governor?" David's cramped hand had been holding a phone all this time — a phone whose screen turned a lovely light blue as David bent his head and pursed his lips as if speaking into a tube. "Tre-von-i-a."

"Dude," I said, "you call your mom 'Trevonia'?"

"Win," he said, "when you're twenty-eight and still living at home, you will call your mother by her first name, too."

"David?" Trevonia said, from the phone in David's lap. Her face, with its bright blue eyes and spidery eyelashes, had appeared on the screen. She looked like a doll whose eyes would close if you pulled a string, and yet the disconcerting thing was that she also had crow's feet and sunburn around her eyes — the eyes of a gardener, the face of a woman who had stared long and hard at life. "David, come to bed, it's late."

"I am sitting here with Win."

"Dear, I don't know who 'Win' is."

"A guy," David said. "Mother hates the fact that all my friends are girls," he said to me. "Mother, Winston is the one —"

"Winston Crwth. Of course," she said. "The boy whose last name rhymes with 'truth.' The boy who was your Scrabble coach.

Please tell Winston that I'd love to meet the two of you for breakfast. But I just took off my face and I'm getting into bed."

"I need my coat," David said. "Win and I are going out to meet
a girlfriend of his."

A deep sigh from David's lap. "Mr. Crwth?" Trevonia said.
"Can you hear me?"

"Yes," I said.

"Speak up," she said.

"I am speaking up," I said. "The phone is on a blanket in
between David's —"

"Mr. Crwth, my son and I are both great admirers. But you
need to promise me that you will get him to bed. As his coach,
you'll appreciate the need for him to get a good night's sleep."

"I am not his coach," I said, in case David and I met in a game
tomorrow and Trevonia wondered why I had betrayed her son. "I
am just —"

She hung up, or David hung up on her by shifting his weight,
and her picture disappeared. "Okay, off we go," he said. "Is this
other girl single?"

He was right about one thing — he was irresistible — and
seemed to think he could go outside without a coat and find Jill
and flirt with her. "Don't you need a coat?" I said.

"It's in mother's room," he said.

"Here," I said, and draped my coat like a blanket on his legs.
Something clonked against his knee and I realized that I had just
given him my frackwater — a stunning mistake that suggested an
inability to think more than one move ahead.

"Um," I said.

"What's the matter — did you want to meet mother and thank
her for your scholarship?"

I reached for the coat — another big mistake as David grabbed the vial and pulled it halfway out and said, "I love vodka. Give me half. Or what is this, Everclear?"

"No, it's Mr. Urlacher's medicine. He needs it," I said, and grabbed the vial with one hand and my coat with the other, splaying my fingers to cover "818" and most of the writing on the top. A lie that came easily because drinking frackwater seemed to be Mr. U's radical cure for something that ailed him, or an expression of some weird need, as the poet of Pennsylvania, to frack himself.

"So he's sick? Don't tell mother. She believes that she should be the next poet laureate."

"He'll be fine. I'll be right back — going to get you a coat."

I got in the elevator with an old man who turned out to be a Scrabbler. I pushed three and he pushed eight, and the old man grinned and said, "Thirty-eighth floor." He called out other floors that did not exist, could not exist, as more people got on and pushed more buttons, until I tried to join the fun by saying, "Minusland."

The old man and his ramblings were weird, a little frightening, but everybody looked at me as if what I'd said was worse. "Minusland is a floor in Willy Wonka's chocolate factory," I said defensively.

"You're that kid who ran out of time and whose score went negative," the old man said to me.

"No," I said, "my score was six."

Mr. U and Thomasina were in their separate beds, their blank faces bathed in the TV's harsh blue light. "Just borrowing a coat," I said, taking Mr. U's coat and walking out and letting the door slam itself shut.

"Win?" I heard through the wood.

"What?" I said.

"Where you going with my coat?" he said.

I thought I was going to meet Linda King LaRue — that the

crippled son of the CEO of Dark Oil & Gas could go to the front of the line and get in to see her — and that Mr. U was better off in bed. "I am going to stand in line."

"What if I decide that I want to stand in line?"

"You drank fracking chemicals," I said quietly.

"And tomorrow — are you going to take my advice about beating David Dark?" Mr. U's crude advice being to hem and haw and hope that David had to go to the bathroom.

"I am," I said. "I'm already playing him."

41

David's wheelchair had gears like a car, and he put it in neutral so that I could push him through the fiery streets of Harrisburg. People held flaming jugs of liquid above their heads and torches that were T-shirts wrapped around branches, sticks. I thought of the scene in *Frankenstein* where people chase the poor monster with their torches and pitchforks. Except in our case the monster was the governor.

LaRue had been a beauty queen, a Miss Northern Tier and a runner-up for Miss Pennsylvania, and there must have been at least ten mannequins riding the shoulders of the mob around the capitol — a few with red paint on their lips, all with eyes the bright blue of burning natural gas, one with a tank on her back and a hose stuck in her head and actual blue flames shooting out of her mouth. Mr. U kept asking me if I'd "know what to do" when I met LaRue, and all I could think of now was to say, "You're beautiful."

A man in the crowd gave David a brown bottle of beer. Another man gave him an orange scarf and wrapped it around his neck. I was about to drape Mr. U's coat around his shoulders when a woman came up and kissed David on the cheek, and it wasn't until another woman sat in his lap and whispered in his ear that I realized David was some kind of celebrity. "Is your father here?" I said.

"Probably inside," he said. "And probably on the phone with Trevonia, asking her what to do. Most men in his position have a bodyguard, a PR firm, and a car on call all day. My dad has a poetess."

"But aren't they divorced?" I said.

"Is that her?" David spotted Jill from a long way away — a shock of long red hair in a field of browns, blacks, and grays.

"Yes, that's her. Her name is Jill."

"What a fox," he said. "Girl like that should just cut in front. Dad would open the door and let her in for sure."

"Your dad's up there with LaRue?"

David told a story about his father's rise through Dark Oil & Gas, something about his father perfecting the technique that let people drill more than a mile underground, then start drilling sideways . . . but I didn't really hear because Jill raised her head and looked at me. A torch lit up her pale face and the scar on her chin looked fresh — as if she'd just cut herself. She held a book and I had a wild fear that it was *Love* and that Mr. U had been standing in line with her.

"Is this the girl?" David said.

"Oh, hi," Jill said to me. "Did you win your tournament?"

"The finals are tomorrow," I said. "You know you're, like, the only person in this line who's reading a book. Everybody else is, like, playing with fire or just staring at their phone —"

"Don't say 'like.'"

"Why not?"

"You're the first cute guy I've seen since lunch. Who talks like a Valley Girl."

"I grew up . . ." I was about to say that I'd grown up in California but didn't want to lie to her. "I grew up in Philadelphia."

"So you read?"

"Just Scrabble," David said unhelpfully.

"That's not reading."

"Right," I said. "So David here knows the governor and says that he can get us in —"

"So what's your favorite book?" she said. "The book so beautiful it hurts?"

Jill had been standing in this line since this morning, and was stomping her feet as if trying to break them out of blocks of ice. But she made me feel like I was the one she'd been waiting to see — that she'd come here to fall in love with me.

"You won't like it."

"Oh?" she said.

"The dictionary."

"Weird." And as if I'd said the one wrong thing and bored a girl who, like Thomasina, seemed to be unboreable, Jill went back to her book. A girl with huge breasts and a bite mark on her neck.

"You drag me all this way and she won't talk to me."

"I'm trying," I said to him. "David knows —"

"Does he know why the water at my house smells like gasoline?" she hissed. "Why my friend's hair is falling out? Does he know why the owls near my house are turning pink?"

"So you know who I am," he said.

"I know you, I know your dad, and I've heard your fracking lies."

"Um," I said, "I don't see how pink owls can be a fracking thing" — a ridiculous sentence that sounded like reading a Scrabble board aloud.

"It's not," David said. "The dead fish are fracking. The pink owls are something else. I'll take it from here if you want to go back to the hotel and rest up for tomorrow."

Now it was my turn to gawp. The night before the biggest

morning of my life — my chance to make Scrabble into something meaningful — David had convinced me to push him into an
angry mob, some of whom were lynching his father in effigy, and
introduce him to a girl who, I knew, must hate him and his family. David kept talking and telling Jill frightening facts about his
family business — that fracking was the cause of earthquakes in
Ohio and bird kills in Arkansas. I kept expecting Jill to fight back
or challenge him, but David's performance was so brazen that she
just stared in disbelief.

"So can I get your number?"

"No."

"You can just speak into this," he said, holding up his phone,
"and it will remember you."

Jill's upper lip was trembling, revealing a broken tooth, and a
white mark on her cheek that must have been a second scar was
now turning red. Jill was in the right, of course, or mostly in the
right, but being right is not enough. And the sight of this strong,
smart, beautiful girl trembling and darkening with rage made
me realize something terrible about LaRue. LaRue was unbeat-
able *because* she was a bad governor — that life under LaRue made
people furious and their fury wore them out.

"Eight-eighteen." This was me, trying to stop the unstoppable
force that was David Dark. "Can your phone remember that?" I
said.

"You're from L.A.? Cool," Jill said.

"How's eight-eighteen possible?"

"I am sorry," David said.

"For what?" Jill said.

"I cheated in a Scrabble game. Something about Scrabble
makes . . . it makes me irresponsible. Thank God I did it in Leah
and not in a real tournament, where I would be banned for life.

Actually, Win, that reminds me — we're trying to buy the rights to drill in Leah and it turns out the best place to sink a well is right on campus, so I've been reaching out to Hale and Leah alumni —"

"Leah is a game?" Jill said.

"Right," he said, "and the damned guy who designed it won't let me frack —"

"Can you die?"

"Of course," he said.

"Horribly?"

"Of course," he said, "but maybe don't kill me till I get you in to see LaRue."

"How?"

"I win the tournament. Does this line move?" he said to her.

"Yes," Jill said, "I think I am two to three days away. It's been slow since they turned the water in the men's room off. So now only women can go in and fill their jugs. But men are coming out with *something* in their jugs — so I'm feeling confident."

"I'll wait, too. Keep you company." David reached behind his back and swished a little black skirt that hung off the back of his chair, revealing a built-in shelf on which I saw a first aid kit, several books, and a box of Triscuits, all shelved horizontally. "Jill, I see you're a fan of paranormal romance and I happen to have —"

"Excuse me," I said to him. "You told me your father is up there with the governor. You said Dark money made LaRue governor. Now you're telling me your plan . . ." It was my plan, too, and seemed idiotic now.

"Dark money with a little *d*," he said. "As in secret. As in corporations are people and any attempt to limit what they can give to Linda King LaRue is a violation of their First Amendment rights."

"Dark Oil and Gas is a person?"

"Yes, in the eyes of the law. Don't blame me. Blame the railroads who in the nineteenth century pioneered the argument that the Fourth Amendment's ban on unreasonable searches and seizures meant the government could not inspect their cars."

"So you're saying . . . So the Bill of Rights . . . What the hell are you saying?"

"I'm saying the Bill of Rights seemed like such a good deal for people, for human beings, that corporations were like, 'Hey, why don't we —'"

"So railroad cars had the same rights as human beings?"

"Probably more, if you were female or African American."

A chilling argument that brought to mind the worst, most Orwellian things I'd read in *The New Soviet Encyclopedia*, such as "A democracy is a form of government in which a minority of the people are ruled by a majority"—a quote that haunted me because it was horrible but also sort of true.

"Can you beat this guy?" Jill said. She had stepped out of line to look up at the sickly green dome of the capitol, a discouraging sight that dimmed the light in her eyes and seemed to make her whole face sag. Then she turned around to look at the thousands of people in line behind us—people who could be days or weeks away from the faucets on the second floor. I stepped out of line so I could stand next to her, and just like that we lost our place, the people stomping, shifting like livestock in a chute.

"I can beat him," David said. "Win's tricky, but I can tell from the way that other girl bamboozled him—"

"I'm talking to Win," she said. "Can you really beat this guy?"

"At Scrabble."

"That's not enough."

I was seventeen and had never voted, and my only trip inside this dome had been disastrous—failing to find my grandfather's old girlfriend, a state senator, because rooms that began with five were all on the second floor, while rooms that began with six were all on the fifth — and I didn't see how I could defeat Dark Oil & Gas.

Jill and I stood uselessly on the cold gray steps, but David still held our place, a scared look on his face as the line pushed his wheelchair forward, back — a look like a mouse being swallowed by a snake.

"I'll wait here," David said, "if you two want to take a break."

"Do you believe him?"

"No," I said.

"Is he safe?"

"Not really, no."

"So it's okay if you want to ask what happened to my face."

"Your chin."

"That's sweet. It's nothing like what happened to those mannequins — those mannekings — the ones with the stitches like Brides of Frankenstein."

"Let me guess. You fought LaRue."

"No," she said, "I slipped and fell. There are lots of people at my school who know more about fracking than me . . . and lots who know more about the sixties and trying to overthrow the government. I'm here because I read and people thought I stood the best chance of getting to the front of the line."

"And you've got me," David said.

Jill looked at him and looked at me, as if trying to make a choice. I draped Mr. U's coat around David's trembling shoulders. Something rustled as I pulled the coat tight around his chest — a receipt, or a love letter, or a wrapper, or a poem that now had a better chance than most of being seen by the governor. I pulled it out, hoping it was Mr. U's great American fracking poem, but, uncrumpling, saw it was blank Hale letterhead. The blank is in some ways the most powerful tile in Scrabble — the tile that grants you a wish — but the sight of this blank piece of paper made me worry that Mr. U had stopped writing because fracking had made him sick.

42

It had been a long day and I needed to sleep. I had suffered the worst defeat in Scrabble history, and had met and didn't think I liked the man who gave me my Dark Scholarship; and I found myself wishing my grandmother was still alive. Nonna was a librarian who worked into her eighties, until she fell and broke her hip. My grandfather put her in a nursing home where she promptly got bronchitis and died before I could get there for a final Scrabble game. Nonna played defensively, tying the board in knots with maddening little words like VAV, her favorite — a style that reminded me of Thomasina.

I walked to the old man's brick apartment building and was about to walk through the cracked, greasy door to the lobby — the pane smeared with so many handprints and fingerprints that it looked like a crime scene — when I saw a word had been scribbled next to CRWTH. The old man had a roommate. Someone with the last name Hooke.

"Grandad?" I said, jabbing at the button by his name.

"Who's there?" a woman said.

"It's his grandson, Winston. Can I speak —"

The door buzzed and I went through and the woman kept speaking while I walked down the hall and knocked on the old man's door. The hall reeked of cigarettes and Nonna would not be pleased to have my grandfather's new roommate or girlfriend stinking up her books. "Come on in," the woman said, opening the door for me. "It took you two tries but you finally found me."

"No," I said, "this is the first time I've been here since —"

"I'm the girl you guys were trying to find on the second floor."

"Excuse me — the girl?" I said. Hooke had a faint gray mustache and her upper lip was curled in a sneer. Her pink tongue trembled, smacked against the roof of her mouth, as if ineffectually trying to say the letter *t*.

"I'm State Senator Charlotte Hooke."

"Oh, you mean the second floor of the capitol where the rooms all start with five."

"A great system, isn't it?"

She looked bad — her hands were trembling and her blouse was misbuttoned so that it rode up around one side of her neck, exposing a pimply white patch of skin around her gut. Hooke with her tics and her misbuttoned blouse looked a lot like someone I would trounce at Scrabble, but she turned out to be my toughest opponent yet. "Your grandfather isn't here. Heard there were free doughnuts at the frackpocalypse. So you're the one at Clovis Friends?" she said.

"No, I'm at the Hale School now."

"Did you know that Clovis Smith was the last man elected to Congress without knowing how to read?" she said.

"Yeah, but how's that possible?"

"Kid," she said, "the coot who chaired the Appropriations Committee before me had to wear an earpiece so the girl in the next room could tell him what to say. It was like the Wizard of Oz if instead of brains and hearts and courage the Wizard gave people heart attacks."

"A girl?" I said.

"Well, me," she said. "I had a head for figures and I didn't mind being behind the curtain, so to speak. Less time getting dressed for work. And that's how I got my start. I could type a hundred-ten words a minute but couldn't get a job as a secretary because of my figure — flat. So I'd be in the back room with a pack of cigarettes and a big pile of WAMs."

"What are WAMs?"

Hooke poured herself a cup of tea and spilled a bit of sugar on her fingers and the table and stuck a finger in her mouth. "WAMs are why my good friends in the senate get confused and think that they are princes, kings."

The world Hooke described seemed so old, so far away — a world of smoke and bad toupees and clattering typewriters — that I guessed WAMs had something to do with men having all the good jobs in Harrisburg while women did all the work. My mother's friends in Berkeley had their own way of spelling "woman," so why not "wam" or "wham" as crude slang for Harrisburg. "Women Against —"

"No," she said. "Walking Around Money. WAMs were supposed to be a way for people to get along. A way for everyone to get what they wanted for their communities — the roads, the bridges, the sewage treatment facilities — without worrying too much where the roads went or if the district had enough shit to merit a facility. But giving people what they want turns out to be dangerous."

"You mean like those stickers that say 'Pennsylvania State Official' and make your car invisible? You mean like Steelers tickets and free trips on the Pennsylvania turnpike and seats on the Dark Oil and Gas jet? You mean like tickets for the Dark skybox at the Cotton Bowl?"

"So you're invisible, too?" she said.

"My friend has one of those stickers on his car," I said, a word I'd never used to describe Thomas Urlacher until meeting Charlotte Hooke and being amazed that Pennsylvania had a poet laureate. Linda King LaRue was terrifying on paper and Charlotte Hooke was terrifying in the flesh, and I began to see how being the poet laureate, how writing poems for these people, would be profoundly depressing.

"So you're a Steelers fan?" she said.

"No, not really, no," I said.

"A muckraker? A fractivist?"

"My roommate writes for the *Derrick*. So I learn a lot from him."

In truth, I knew about the Dark jet and the Dark skybox because a guy on Fitler's second floor played squawking talk radio so loudly that other guys had called the show and tried to get through with a plausible question about fracking or the Steelers — the real goal being to say, "Dude, turn down your radio."

"So by WAMs you mean freebies, things like tickets —"

"Chicken feed," Hooke sneered at me. "I mean money for a football stadium. I mean money for a bridge to nowhere and a road to Coudersport. A skating rink which made the state senator in the next county so mad that he got a skatium. A shooting range for some faggoty version of the Boy Scouts, like the Boy Scouts but with fags, and a dunk tank and a new, child-friendly stage and gallows for the Renaissance Faire. A new statue of William Penn for our sister city in East Anglia because the old statue turned out to be flammable. The world's first underground miniature golf course and its third gumball museum. A ten-year, multimodal study of Philadelphia's transportation needs which got scrapped so we could buy a bus that will take people to the new waterfront casinos. A study on the benefits of expanding legalized gambling which involved giving a state senator's wife money to go gambling. A twenty-year appropriation for the Longevity Center, which is a nice way of saying 'the Museum of Old People' and a very nice way of saying 'Pennsylvania.' WAMs are like wishes and I was the darling of all those Dark lobbyists . . . all except for the Bitch."

"Who's the Bitch?"

"LaRue," she said. "Somehow LaRue got a list of every single WAM and she blamed them all on me. There's no real paper trail with WAMs, so it's hard to prove that for every wish I granted — like building a casino at Valley Forge — there were even stupider wishes where we all said no. WAMs are bad but people forget that I was the only thing between us and SWAMPs."

"What are SWAMPs?"

"They're like WAMs, but in perpetuity."

I yawned. "Perpetuity" is the kind of word I love — a long word for something long — but I was exhausted and could not keep up with her. "Can I stay —"

"Ask your grandfather." Hooke smacked my wish back like a floating Ping-Pong ball — putting it away before it had even crossed the net.

"Please," I said, "I'm in the round of thirty-two in this Scrabble tournament, and the winner gets to go up and meet the governor, and I'm thinking that I'll beat her by —"

Hooke winced. "I like 'beat' but not the Scrabble part. Tell me what you mean by 'beat.' LaRue plays in this tournament?"

"No, she plays whoever wins. Probably it's just a photo op, and for all I know she has someone play her words for her —"

"Tell me what you mean by 'beat.'"

"Defeat."

"Impossible. Once they're in, they're in," she said. "Pennsylvania is a state where it takes years for people to admit they've made mistakes, a lifetime to correct them. We don't unelect governors."

"Expose —"

"Is this going to be like the time she threw out the first pitch at a Phillies game and the catcher, a Democrat, let it hit him in the face? The people who chained themselves to the Ben Franklin Bridge to protest the use of gasoline? The caller who got through to her by pretending to be Nancy Reagan, and talked to her about being a Cancer in a way that made it sound like LaRue was making fun of people with cancer, and then put the whole thing up on the Internet?"

"Tell the tru—"

"Or is it going to be like the time ten thousand people surrounded the capitol and stood in line for days to fill their Starbucks cups with water from LaRue's toilet?"

"Senator, forgive my ignorance, but I don't see what those things have in com—"

"They didn't work! And Linda King LaRue is more popular than ever."

I kept trying to explain why it was so important for me to meet LaRue. I had promised Mr. U that I would talk to her about his poetry. I promised the Feldkircher kid that I would ask LaRue about their milk and the tests that said their water was safe. And deep down I had the ugly thought that, if I lost my nerve and couldn't talk about fracking with her, LaRue was a good person to know in case I lost my Dark Scholarship.

I had a plan—a better plan than waiting in line for days—but could not get more than one or two words out before Hooke would object and spit them back in my face. Every word I said could be used to describe some other foolish attempt to challenge LaRue or some other governor, and it was like I had to come up with the best plan to challenge the Pennsylvania Powers That Be in history and had to describe it in two words or less.

"Fracking."

Hooke's face went slack. Her teacup stopped clattering.

"I have proof that fracking is really, really dangerous."

A mistake. Hooke was hard to read but I should have known she would have heard these words before. "Dangerous is what people said about cars without seat belts. Dangerous is what people said about secondhand smoke. And do you know how many million people had to die before —"

"This is worse. A cigarette can't light water on fire —"

"I'm from Pittsburgh. I have seen an entire river burn."

"Fracking is —"

Hooke flinched as if her tea was scalding hot. It went on and on like this — Hooke shooting me down because my facts, my arguments, my choice of words had all been tried and failed before. Saying "fracking" might make her blush and shut up momentarily. But I went to this well one too many times and lost my power over her, and wound up listening to a long story about Hooke's mentor in politics, a delegate from Maryland whose greatest accomplishment had been getting a women's bathroom put in the state capitol building in Annapolis. Talking to Hooke was like playing some maddening version of Scrabble in which words could be used only once . . . or like writing for Mr. U when he made us write without using nouns or verbs.

I couldn't outthink Hooke and couldn't get two words out . . . until the musty smell of my grandmother's books brought back a memory of sitting in front of her fire, drinking warm milk and feeling my face get hot like a baked potato. I yawned uncontrollably.

"You poor kid," Hooke said in a softer tone of voice. "I'm a lot tougher than LaRue. Beat me and chances are that you can beat her, too. What's your plan? I mean let's say —"

I put on my coat. The jar of frackwater clonked against my collarbone, and while I was tempted to pull it out and hand it to her wordlessly, Hooke had picked up the phone and was already helping me.

"Hello, dear, it's Charlotte Hooke. I need a room for one, for Crwth. Oh, what bad luck. Winston, I'm . . . are suites more expensive?"

"Eight-eighteen," I blurted out. "Is eight-eighteen available?"

"Did you hear that? Yes, we want eight-one-eight, if possible. Winston like Churchill and Crwth with a *w*. But the whole thing rhymes with 'truth.'"

43

Snow fell on Jill and David and the thousands of other people waiting to see LaRue while I slept in my warm, soft king bed. I had put my mad Scrabble plan before my friends — abandoning Thomasina in a room with Mr. U, abandoning Jill with David Dark, or, perhaps, him with her. Hard to say which of them would make the other more miserable — the girl fighting the fracking happening near her house, or David Dark, the son and heir of Dark Oil & Gas. But I slept beautifully in suite 818 and now felt like the prince who peeks through his curtains at sunrise and gives thanks to God that he is not a commoner.

Snow covered the green dome like sugar sprinkled on a cake. People swarmed the capitol like so many hungry ants — streaming up the steps to the main entrance and the chocolate double doors, climbing on a derrick built right under LaRue's window. Flames shot out the top, and the head — the part that looks like the head of a mule — was chunking up and down as if the capitol were being fracked. The sight was thrilling, as if a conquering army had come to overthrow the governor, an army bearing torches from all over Pennsylvania. I thought of Valley Forge and Washington's army surviving on fire cakes — a name that implied something wonderful, a food that filled your belly and made your whole body warm, until my father told me that a fire cake was just a simple mixture of flour and water, and that thousands of soldiers had starved to death because Congress could not be bothered to feed them.

The First Fracking Army of Pennsylvania seemed to have at

least ten thousand soldiers, and I wondered if they had a general and weapons besides torches and the toxic chemicals collected from their backyards and their kitchen sinks. There were at least twice as many people in the streets and camped out on the capitol grounds as there had been yesterday, but the line of people waiting to see LaRue or get water from her bathroom seemed to have disappeared in places . . . until I looked more closely and saw that parts of the line now had walls and an intermittent roof, and chairs and other furniture — all as if they were hunkering down to spend the winter here.

My room faced north and east and I could see several hundred tents pitched in the streets; parked cars had become the walls of drafty little forts whose other walls were blankets, boxes, plastic crates, bales of bundled newspapers. Wooden rungs had been nailed to the trunk of a tree and people were climbing up to sit in a kind of crude tree house. Mr. U and Thomasina's room was down on the third floor — close enough to see the protesters shivering and hear them moaning in the cold. From the eighth floor, in the soft pink light of morning, the army looked enormous, strong, unstoppable, except for one confusing fact: the bright blue flame of Dark Oil & Gas appeared on many of these tents, several signs, and a flag, as if Dark had taken pity and did not want these people to freeze to death. As if Dark was somehow on their side and sick of Linda King LaRue.

44

I took a long, hot shower and got French toast, bacon, and coffee delivered to my room. "Charge it all to Charlotte Hooke," I said.

The old man who'd brought my food beamed at this and seemed to understand, but then said, "Charge it to your room? Or just charge it all to Dark?"

"What?" I said.

"Eight-eighteen is the Dark Suite and I presume you'd like —"

"I am not with Dark," I said automatically. "Wait — you're saying this room belongs to Dark Oil and Gas?"

"King herself stayed here when she was on Dark's board of directors."

"Why 'King'? Why not 'LaRue'?"

"Because she was Linda King before she married the first gentleman."

"So who's he?"

"Dark's attorney."

"Did they live here?"

"Briefly, yes, a sort of working honeymoon."

"Have you ever seen this many people in Harrisburg?"

"No, not since the meltdown at Three Mile Island."

I gave him two bucks — all I had — and ate by the window, scanning the crowd for David in his wheelchair, or a girl with bright red hair. David must have had a better plan than waiting in line all night — after all, his father was one of LaRue's biggest campaign contributors — but Jill had a masochistic streak and seemed like the kind of girl who would rather wait than cut.

I drank more coffee in the lobby and felt giddy, confident. My first game would be against David and I guessed he'd stayed out late, trying to win a girl who seemed to hate him and his family. There were thirty-two players left and our names had been written on brackets that branched out horizontally from the word CHAMPION. Scrabble had wrecked the way I read — scanning an entire page before reading it line by line, reading vertically so that I knew what would happen next, without understanding why — and yet I failed to read these brackets from right to left and failed to see that, among the people I might have to play in the finals, was a guy with the last name Ha.

Our chairs had been draped with ads for Dark Oil & Gas. I stared at the bright blue flame while waiting for David. Beating him would be terrible but a forfeit would be worse. I sat with my head in the dictionary until I heard the crinkling — the ads were as brittle, cheap, and disposable as the paper on a doctor's examination table — of someone sitting across from me.

"Where's my son?"

"He met a girl," I said. I could not bear to look Trevonia in the eyes — to face the fury of my guardian angel.

"In the bar?"

My mouth opened. I made a sound as if swallowing a piece of wood.

"David is a grown man and it's none of my business," Trevonia said. "I just want to know if he's going to forfeit and if the last three years of driving him to these stupid tournaments will have been for nothing."

"He met a girl in the line to see LaRue."

"Jesus Christ. A fractivist? His father will kill me."

"Yes, I'm sorry, yes," I said.

Trevonia smiled. "That's actually very *Richard the Third*, don't you think? 'She cannot choose but hate thee.'"

I had left her son in the freezing cold all night and now I was flinging my scholarship in her face. Desperately, I tried to think of something I could say or do to make it up to her. "Scrab?" I said.

She shook her head.

"Does this mean —"

"You've lost my vote? That's exactly what it means. But I'll be as straight with you as you have been with me. David also gets a vote, and his father gets a vote, so there's no reason why you can't win another scholarship. Maybe this girl you've found will make my son happy. And maybe you'll turn out to be one of Dark's real champions."

"Mrs. Dark, I'm sorry, but David told me something about fracking that I can't —"

"Is this the flaming water?"

"No."

"The earthquakes in Ohio?"

"No, it's that David's trying to buy the rights to drill in a computer game. I mean it seems to me you guys have some things to sort out in Pennsylvania before you start —"

"You're confused. When I say you could be one of our real champions, I mean win the tournament. Dark Scholars have gone on to do wonderful things in medicine, in archaeology, and while I know that Scrabble can't really be called a 'field,' wouldn't it be marvelous —"

"Mrs. Dark, I'm sorry."

"Why?"

"I can't be your champion."

45

My next opponent was another babbler. A young man with rosebud lips, a painfully short haircut, and a tremor in one hand that made the bag of tiles shake and made him drop one on the floor.

"Don't," Thomasina said, as I bent to pick it up. You are not allowed to touch your opponent's tiles and can be disqualified.

"Thanks," I said, and turned around to see her playing a nun. A day after giving me the worst beating in Scrabble history, Thomasina sounded like she was on my side again.

I beat the babbler handily and Thomasina beat the nun, and it turned out that "Wodtke-Weird," as I heard the nun muttering under her breath, was my next opponent. "Scrab?" she said, and smiled at me. Her face was puffy and her eyes were bloodshot. "Sorry to bark at you but I've been trying to get your attention all morning. Finally, I figured the best way was to win my game and force you to sit across from me."

"I was busy —"

"Scrabbling while I was taking Mr. U to the hospital. You mean you didn't get my text?"

"No phones," said an old man whose bright blue hat and blue T-shirt identified him as a judge.

"Or didn't you get Rich's text?"

The judge had an aquiline nose and was staring right at us. TILDEN HAYES, his nametag read — a name my dad would love because no one really knows who got the most votes and who was the real winner in 1876 — Samuel J. Tilden or Rutherford B. Hayes.

Tilden blinked in disbelief as I pulled my phone out and discovered it was dead. "That's one," he said to me. "Say, 'One what?' that will be two. No talking. No touching. No funny stuff like yesterday."

A crowd gathered to watch this rematch of the lowest-scoring and one of the most humiliating games in history, and this was unfortunate because, for once, the only girl at Hale needed my help desperately. "So, listen, the good news is that Tom got his stomach pumped and is doing a lot bet —"

"That's one," Tilden said to her.

"And the really good news is that he finished his poem this morning and they've asked him to read it at the rally this afternoon —"

"That's two," he said to her. "Other people trying to play."

"Thomasina — please," I hissed. "Do not get disqualified." I had already won a game by forfeit, when David did not appear, and it would look suspicious if I kept beating people without actually playing them. Thomasina frowned and looked like she was going to speak. Cruel as she'd been with Rich — letting him bring her nouns and hope that she'd perform his verbs — volatile as she'd been with his father, and combative as she'd been with me, I had always blamed these things on the fact that Thomasina was the only girl at the Hale School. The alternative was worse, too terrible to contemplate — that she went to Hale *because* she was cruel and liked being around boys who were dumb and scared of her. My first instinct had been right — to leave her with Mr. U — except that Mr. U had cast some new spell over her and all she wanted to do was talk about his masterpiece. "It's deep," she said. "It's amazing. You are going to love it, Win."

"Shh," I said. A word had been challenged in another game — a word played by an Asian kid who looked vaguely familiar — and Tilden was flipping through the pages of his dictionary. "Is this three?" he said to Thomasina.

THIS she played on her next turn. IS she played on her next. She was beating me on points and I now had a hell of a time trying to win our game while preventing her from playing THREE. I had the remaining H and could have played SHH but knew this would anger her. She played a dirty word and some things that weren't words and I didn't challenge them. I just wanted to win and do so before she dragged me down with her.

I eked out a win and signed my name on my scorecard and would have been all ears until my next game — eager to hear about Mr. U, his masterpiece, and their trip to the hospital — except that Thomasina looked sick to her stomach.

"What?" I said.

"I just realized who that Asian kid is. Peter Ha. The brother of that guy who killed himself."

46

Peter Ha heard his name and took off his sunglasses. Peter had deep-set eyes and a dazed look like he'd been driving all night. He had reddish, blotchy skin and I now remembered that Alivert — a kind of acne medication that gave kids wild mood swings — had been blamed for his brother's suicide.

None of which frightened me. I thought coming to Harrisburg with my jar of frackwater and my plan to bring down Linda King LaRue was clever and a good reason — karmically speaking — for me to win the tournament. Better even than winning it to avenge your brother who won it, then killed himself. No, the thing that frightened me happened right after I won my next-to-last game of the tournament — against a really old guy who told me that he used to play bingo before Scrabble was invented — which was also the next-to-next-to-last game of my life. Peter Ha smiled at me — a big, friendly grin that made him seem warm, happy, and almost profoundly sane. And while Peter may simply have been a friendly guy, or may have liked me instinctively, giving his smile extra watts, something about his warmth, his handsomeness, his aura of *togetherness* was far more frightening than anything I'd faced so far. I had felt superior to the ten-year-old girl who played HAOLE until I played HAOLES in order to beat her. I was horrified by Barbara's babbling, but that's the way I sounded when playing against myself. I let Thomasina toy with me, and only beat David Dark by physically wheeling him away from the tournament and leaving him outside all night — and knew I was as bad or worse than any of my opponents. Peter frightened me because he seemed like a nice, normal guy who was just here having fun.

"The man himself," Peter said, as I sat across from him. I had never been called a "man" before — not even by a friend kidding around because, of course, I barely had any friends — and this also unnerved me.

"I'm sorry?"

"The man who got the lowest score in history. The man who seems to be friends with the first good-looking girl that I have ever seen at a Scrabble tournament. The man who people tell me is from Philly and San Fran and has some kind of east-west, yin-yang magic to his game." Peter's flattery went straight to my head and made it hard to concentrate — and even made me wonder if, more than winning, more than the respect of Mr. U or Thomasina or the other boys at Hale, all I'd needed was love.

"Yeah," I said, "my parents thought it would make me cosmo-politan."

"Did it?"

"No — I think I got the worst aspects of each coast."

"Too hot, too cold?"

"A hippie prig."

Peter laughed. A siren song that would dash me on the rocks. Was he from California, too? The land of hope, of happiness? I liked him enormously and was disappointed when we had to play our game. We had really hit it off and couldn't stop talking and both got "two" from Tilden Hayes so quickly that it seemed like our sudden friendship would get us disqualified. Peter even threw away a chance to turn DJINN into DJINNS or DJINNI so that he could answer something I'd asked earlier:

SENIOR

I had asked how old he was and where he went to school, and this must have meant he was a college senior. These are six of the most common letters in the bag — and six with which it is fairly easy to make a seven-letter word — so that communicating with me was a real sacrifice. I wanted to respond in kind but also couldn't shake the thought that this was some kind of trick. But maybe it had to do with his brother's memory — the fact that his brother, before he died, had spelled out a cry for help. Maybe I struck Peter as another lost Scrabble soul and maybe he had come here, not to win, but to save someone like me.

He played brilliantly and had such a happy, intelligent face —

two qualities I used to think were contradictory — that I wanted to know his secret. Had he always played like me, or had he only picked it up after Stephen killed himself? I'd been playing this damned game almost every day since I was four or five — more than ten thousand games against people, computers — and if I'd never met someone I liked more than the game itself, neither had I met someone who was so much nimbler. And the combination of these two things was thrilling, humbling — like climbing a hill that turns out to be a mountain.

The end of most games tends to be miserable — the board so clogged with words that it can be hard to go, the feeling that you are being forced to live with all of your mistakes. Peter was so far ahead that I would probably need to play two or three seven-letter words in a row. AAEEURT, my hand screamed at me. I had less than a minute left on my clock and would also lose if I ran out of time and started to go negative.

"'Aureate,'" I said, and played this word on the board, finding the gold in what seemed like dross.

"'Laureate,'" he said at once, and played for so many points that I would need some other way of beating him besides getting the highest score. I could try to get him to speak or break some other rule. I could try to explain that I had come too far and suffered too much *not* to win this tournament and that he should let me win. I could reach into my shirt and clonk my frackwater on the table, but the only thing big enough for him to read — SUITE CODE 818 — might seem completely meaningless.

Asking another player to cheat is itself cheating, and if Tilden Hayes caught me, or if anyone looking at our game now, or in the newspaper, or online, or, hearing about my increasingly erratic play, saw that I'd been trying to cheat, I would be banned for life. I looked at my rack one last time and actually had a seven-letter word — GLYCYLS — but nowhere for it to go.

CHEAT I played, with the C on HEAT.

A terrible thing to do. Everybody failed to see his brother writing in a game and there seemed to be no way they could make this mistake again. Peter would be banned for life if he cheated for my sake, and I would be banned for asking him to cheat, although — and this was my hope — maybe Peter would understand that I must have a really, really good reason to take such a drastic step. Usually, he didn't look at my tiles as I played them. He was the kind of player who "kept" the board in his head. But he looked at CHEAT now and so gave himself away.

"Pass," he said — a perfectly respectable thing to do, but one that prolonged our game and gave me a chance to put LA in front of RUE.

"Challenge," Peter said. "Larue" is not a word and I knew that I would lose. "Larue" might be a word eventually — the way "sandwiches" were named for the Earl of Sandwich — but for now it was the only way to explain why he should cheat — the only word that summed up why winning was so important, or, okay, the only one I could play right then and there.

I lost. Peter didn't cheat. And I would be banned for life. There was no other way to read a kid playing CHEAT and LARUE with a chance to meet LaRue at stake.

"Nice game," Peter said. "The answer to your question is that I'm a senior at UC Berkeley. So give me a call sometime when you're in California."

I slipped the jar of frackwater out of my pants pocket and thought about pouring it on the floor. But the board was all the evidence Tilden Hayes would need to ban me from Scrabbledom. He sat down across from me and began copying the words in our game, his silence more damning than "that's three" or anything else he could say. I had lost, not just a game, but Scrabble itself, and did not know what to do. I had lost my chance to fight for

Jill, my school, for the Feldkirchers, for everyone who'd been fracked.

I couldn't feel my feet and had begun to cry when Peter tapped me on the back. "It's for you," he said, and handed me a phone.

"Hello?" I said.

"Winston Crwth," she said. "This is Linda King LaRue. Congratulations. I can't tell you how much we could use some good news around here."

"You could?"

"I've got the *Inky* and you're going to be famous. You're my hero. With all the problems we've been having here today — trying to feed all these people and trying to keep them warm — I can't tell you how happy it makes me to think a Dark Scholar would win our little tournament and put things into perspective."

"But I didn't win," I said. "I came in second. I've been dis —"

"Mr. Ha declined to be in a photograph with me. So it looks like you're our man."

47

CHEAT was cheating. Being a Dark Scholar meant that I was the wrong person to clonk a jar of frackwater on her desk. And the fact that several hundred of the several thousand people thronging the capitol were now sitting in flimsy orange chairs with DARK on the back — the flames suggesting a football team called the Pennsylvania Dark — or eating hot dogs, hamburgers, and bright blue popsicles being served from Dark trucks, or huddling in Dark tents with Styrofoam cups of hot chocolate, or standing around huge, humming space heaters that were covered with grease, sand, oil, and sticky stuff like Vaseline, or, worst of all, the fact that a lot of the children here were now sledding down a hill in bright orange

Dark flyers made me think the Fracking Army had already lost the war. The whole thing had taken on the air of a carnival and it was hard to hear the chants of the protesters through a watery roar and a high-pitched, maddening hiss. Among the things for sale in the pages of the *Derrick* were "antinoise" machines, which seemed to work by disrupting the sound waves coming from other machinery, and I wondered if Dark had tuned one like a radio to disrupt the speech, the thoughts, of all of these fractivists.

"What's that awful sound?" I asked a middle-aged man wearing a Yale windbreaker with the *l* shaped like an oar.

"The Johnstown Flood."

"Is that a band?"

"A heavy metal band from West Virginia."

"Are they for or against fracking?"

"What?"

"I said is the Johnstown Flood for or against —"

Feeling less cool than a middle-aged Ivy Leaguer in a crew windbreaker is depressing, and that is how I felt after this one scolded me. "Listen and I think you'll understand that these guys are beyond concepts like 'for' and 'against.'"

I didn't see Jill, David, or my grandfather on the steps, so I walked up to the front of the line to get into the building — achieving in seconds what might take hours, days, for the other people here — and said my name to a man with a clipboard and a tightly holstered gun.

"Go right in, Mr. Crwth," he said. "The governor is expecting you."

The shrieking, grinding hiss of the Johnstown Flood was louder inside the building so that, whatever their views on fracking, the band was making it hard for either side to think. David was parked behind an information desk, his wheelchair shaking with the bass. He sat stooped, speaking loudly into the phone in his lap. A half-empty bottle of Spuyten Duyvil Double IPA was in his good hand and an empty bottle and steaming cup of coffee were stuck between his thighs. I'd been feeling bad about leaving him to freeze, but he had the most wonderful expression on his face — the disbelief of a kid on Christmas morning — and far from freezing, David seemed to have been partying.

"'Escheat,'" he said to me. "You know you could have played 'escheat' and would have had a chance to win."

A lie but a nice thing to say. "I cheated. I'll be banned for life."

"So what? I was banned *from* life at birth and you don't hear me complaining."

The shame of what I'd done was just beginning to sink in, and I was so grateful to David for saying this that I decided to bring him with me. A guy who could forgive me and still be my friend despite my weakness, my selfishness, would be useful in a meeting with the governor. "Where is Jill?"

He rolled his eyes as if commenting on the hopelessness of finding Jill, the hopelessness of going out with her.

"David, I'm sorry if I got you in trouble with Trevonia."

"You're in worse. You can forget about another scholarship. Did you find a place to stay?" A cruel way of putting this — as if my place in Hale was already in jeopardy — but mostly he was asking if I'd found a place to sleep.

"In the Dark Suite, actually, the Dark Suite at the Hilton."

"Nice," he said. "You know that's where Linda and my dad and I hung out before she was governor. The Dark Suite is where I had my first drink and kissed my first girl and did X. Don't do X. And it's where Linda got her big idea for a way to test water safely."

I did not like the sound of this. LaRue was not a scientist, and "safely" seemed to mean "hide the fact that water was dangerous."

I remembered driving up to Hale for the first time and seeing all the freakishly green grass around the wells and deciding I did not want to know about fracking. That kid would have heard the weird, Orwellian "test water safely" and not worried about the meaning, and, instead, would have rearranged these letters to get "we try safe lattes" or something else ridiculous, hiding the truth from himself.

"Is your father here?" I said.

"He's manning the grill," he said.

"At what, a fund-raiser?"

"No," he said, "in the tent we set up to give all these people breakfast. Like you, my father is increasingly concerned about Governor LaRue's inability to strike a balance between protecting the environment and promoting the responsible use of our natural resources. Just because we are the Saudi Arabia of natural gas doesn't mean we need to behave like Saudi Arabia when . . ."

His words were drowned out by the Flood, drumming and a scream like a demon who had stubbed his toe. David was still talking; and if it's true that I heard enough to guess that something was up and that the ground had shifted under LaRue, with the CEO of Dark Oil & Gas making pancakes for the mob, it is also true that David's speech bored me and that I just didn't care.

"David, I don't know how long you have been sitting here, and I don't know what you saw last night —"

"I saw a girl with red hair and lips like *sakura masu.*"

"— but 'these people' are a mob and they hate your family!" I yelled, trying to make myself heard over a sound like a violin being played with a knife.

David shrugged. "Well, they seem to like our hot chocolate. Dad's outside. Why don't we go talk about your scholarship?"

A choice between turning back and trying to save myself, and heading upstairs to save Pennsylvania. I had been inside for no more than five minutes and the Flood had given me a ringing in one ear.

"Up here, dummy."

Jill had been here all night and had been listening to the Flood all morning and had timed this perfectly so that I could hear her — calling me a dummy at the exact moment when the band seemed to pause for breath. She stood in the line that went up the wide marble steps to LaRue's office on the second floor. She was holding a milk jug. "Bring me anything good to read?" This line I got by reading her lips.

"Yes!" I said, despite the fact I had not brought anything. I hated Rich's philosophy of pretty girls — that being pretty made them crazy — and yet I had just lied again because Jill was a girl for whom I would do anything, for whom I could *find* something good to read in the next few seconds. "David, listen, I would love to meet with your father and talk about my scholarship, but right now I have got a meeting with LaRue. Want to come?"

"You're kidding. How?"

"I lied, cheated, sold my soul" would have been accurate. "Scrabble."

"That's incredible. Bringing Jill?"

"Of course," I said.

David put his chair in gear and drove himself to an elevator that said MEMBERS ONLY. "I'll meet you guys at the top."

"I need this," I said, and snatched the phone from between his legs, spilling coffee and some beer as he tried to snatch it back. I looked quickly at the screen, expecting to see Scrabble, or, perhaps, his mother's face, but what I saw was worse: an article about fracking chemicals turning up in drinking water as far away as Baltimore.

The phone was black and so slick that it almost flew out of my hands as I ran up the stairs. I was out of breath as Jill kissed me on the cheek and I wound up breathing hotly in her ear. She was older and I thought she'd know how to kiss or what to do, but, like me, seemed confused about where our noses went. This is how I skipped kissing her and went straight to biting her white earlobe, and heard this thrilling girl moan in pain but mostly in pleasure.

"So," she said, and grabbed my shirt as if to keep from falling down, "I'm almost to the top and then we can fill this thing and go get some lunch."

"Come with me — I got us a meeting with the governor."

"No way. How?"

"Dishonestly."

She kissed me and got my lower lip between her teeth as if she might bite down hard. I had never understood how a girl could like me for my flaws. "Ow," she said as we hugged, the jar of frack-water hard and cold between us.

"Here," I said, and pulled it out, "I brought you something good to read."

"What is this?"

"A jar of water from a fracked dairy farm."

"How romantic."

"Also this," handing her David's phone. "It's David's."

"I know," she said. "I just spent all night being emailed, tweeted, called, filmed, googled, photographed."

"And?"

"David has decided that I'm an English major, not an ecoterrorist."

She put the phone and the water in her purse and held my hand as we walked to the top of the stairs. Here the line seemed to split in two, with nine or ten men with the blackest, shiniest shoes that I had ever seen standing in front of a door that said:

GOVERNOR LINDA KING LARUE

And with a lot more people with jugs, bottles, jerry cans, even empty beer bottles standing in front of a door with this symbol:

"Where's the men's room?" I asked Jill.

"The men broke it."

"Oh," I said.

The contrast between these two doors said it all to me—one door for the shiny shoes waiting to see LaRue, one door for the rest of us. Some of the people waiting for water from the women's room sprawled on the ground with backpacks and duffel bags and Dark chairs and sleds they'd grabbed before entering the building, looking like victims of a natural disaster. But if they looked wrecked and exhausted at first glance, a lot of them were smiling and talking animatedly, while others wore the blank, ecstatic look of mountaineers who had almost reached the peak. The sight of an old man coming out of this women's room with a bottle of water raised triumphantly above his head made me think the Fracking Army might win the war—or, if not win the war, then have the better tale to tell—for many of the men waiting to see LaRue herself looked stiff and frozen like people waiting for a bus. And while some of these men looked almost comically miserable—with jowls that made them look like confused, disappointed dogs and with big, flabby barrel chests, which in one case was clearly being held in place by a girdle—none looked like he had been waiting in this line all night. So while I'd learned a thing or two about Pennsylvania politics and knew, for example, that people in the capitol played by their own set of rules and had stickers that made their cars invisible, and that the state poet laureate was expected to be the Bard of Oil and Gas, and that even people whose *water caught on fire* had a hard time getting the government's attention and had to wait in line for days, I now saw with cold fury that even this line was a lie and that a bottle of tap water was, for these people, the most they were going to get from Linda King LaRue.

48

I knocked on her door. I didn't see David and thought he must be inside. People were staring and I began to worry that the truth about my cheating had gotten to the governor, or that she or somebody was about to call my bluff. I looked at David's phone and tried to appear nonchalant. He had several emails from Ian Dark, his father, and a single text that said:

congrats son this jill girl sounds like a fox a fox in heat

"Open the door," David said. He'd rolled up behind us and was barely audible above the Flood. But the door swung open and she must have been expecting him. The lobbyist with the girdle was elbowing by me and grabbing the handles of David's wheel-chair — as if David's driver would also be admitted — and while I felt confident that I could handle LaRue, the flushed look of fear, shame, and determination on this man's face frightened and embarrassed me. A look like Rich's when I'd walked in on him once with his cock in his hands.

"Governor?" this man said to her. "I know you don't have time for all of us, but Ian Dark and I would like —"

"Not your turn," she said to him.

"I —"

"Although I like your new haircut. Very navy."

"Now I look like my nine navy pals."

"What?" she said.

"You told me once that 'nine navy pals' is an anagram —"

"You look navy but you're sounding like the captain of the *Titanic*."

"The movie or the play?"

"The boat."

"So it's women and children first? Governor, I just need two —"

"Two or to or too?" she said. "I've got David's dad flipping pancakes for the mob and I've got you stalking me and I think you Dark boys need to get your story straight."

The man did not respond to this; a lump like a wad of tobacco in his mouth was, in fact, his tongue prodding, probing something stuck between his teeth. "It's okay," David said to him. "My dad told me to handle things." And in the same way he'd assumed that I would be his friend, and that Jill would be his girlfriend, and that he and his dad could handle the mob and carry the day for Dark Oil & Gas, David smiled and closed the door on this obscene-looking man. Then he turned around and sighed as if this were his office, too.

"I'm not a child," I said to her.

"Excuse me?"

"The thing about women and children first."

"Ah, but you're the Scrabble Kid. Come on in. We've only got a few minutes before my next appointment."

"I'm with him," Jill said to her.

"I don't have time for that," she said, as if Jill had meant "with" dirtily. "David, did you want to be in the picture, too?"

"With two foxes? Sure," he said. I fought the urge to tell him that a female fox is a vixen. LaRue seemed fond of him and might not understand our relationship, in which David got the taunting and tough love some people would not give a guy in a wheelchair. I took his empty coffee cup and two empty beer bottles, and stood there holding them because there was no trash can. A single, empty bottle on one of LaRue's bookshelves had a stopper and looked like it had been salvaged from a shipwreck. Also on her shelves were *Love* and some of Mr. U's other books, a copy of the dictionary from which, I knew, he'd lifted his lines about love, seven or eight copies of *The Lorax*, a bound copy of Ben Franklin's *Poor Richard's Almanack*, a book called *Law School for Dummies* shelved next to the annotated code of Pennsylvania from 1957, and a lot of pictures of LaRue doing things like driving a pickup, shoveling snow off a roof, coaching a girls' soccer game in the rain, and posing in her bikini as Miss Northern Tier.

"Where do I —"

"I keep asking people for a trash can as a gift, but they don't believe me. What to get the woman who has everything."

"And knows it all," David said. "How many beauty queens go on to get a Ph.D.?"

"None. That says 'Ph.T.,'" she said. "My husband made that one for me."

"Ph.T.?"

"Put hubby through."

"The wall?" Jill said.

"I wish," she said.

I liked her office and liked her more than I thought I would. She didn't seem bothered in the least by the sound of the Flood or thousands of people chanting her name angrily, and seemed to do her job as governor the way I had been a Scrabbler: make the best of things and solve one problem at a time.

"Where's the *Inky*?" I needed to humiliate her utterly and thought it wouldn't matter if I didn't have an audience.

"He left when you weren't the brother of the guy who killed himself. But they'll run something if we do all the work and come up with a cute photograph."

"Where's your staff?"

"I wanted to speak with David privately," she said, opening a drawer beneath the bookshelf and pulling out a Scrabble board on which several words had already been played — words like SCHOOLS and ROADS and POLICE and HOUSING and TRANS-PORTATION. "Winston, do you know what I love about Scrabble?"

"What?"

"No punctuation. I can do this one thing but don't have time for questions."

"I have one," Jill said to her. "Why does the women's room have a picture of a woman with one leg?"

"Because only Nixon could go to China."

A line that made David grin but flummoxed me. "This won't do," I said to her, pointing at the board. "There aren't this many Os. The whole thing looks kind of fake."

"Winston, this is how it works. Even on the best of days I can't actually go for a run, or eat my lunch, or play a game of Scrabble. I just need it to look like we were Scrabbling."

"It's still not good enough — not even as a fake."

"Fix it."

I dumped the board upside down and some of the tiles fell on the floor. LaRue got down on her knees and picked them up for me like I was a helpless child, and I began to wonder if I had misjudged her. "It's okay if it looks fake because the roads and the new schools and wastewater treatment facilities will be real enough if I get my fracking tax," she said, her words sounding hollow because she'd stuck her head under a chair in order to chase a D. "Every other state has one and every other state is getting rich —"

"Win," David said, "play your game and let's get out of here.

It's not too late for you to grab a few minutes with my dad. Linda here has already been more than generous."

"Also," Jill said to her, her lower lip trembling, "why do you have so many copies of *The Lorax*?"

"Sweetheart—what happened to your ear?" LaRue said, alarmedly. A dark bruise where I'd bitten her.

"My ear?" Jill said.

"You didn't have that bite when you were in line last night."

"You were in—"

"Not in the line, but I walked right by you on my way in to work this morning. You were reading your book and must not have noticed me."

"Good God," Jill said, "that's embarrassing." Like me, she had come here because LaRue was the face of fracking and seemed to have the power to make fracking less dangerous; and, like me, Jill seemed mesmerized by the fact that LaRue was smart, funny, and *human*, not some Bride of Frankenstein.

"I have so many copies of *The Lorax* because I get one as a gift in, oh, in about two percent of the meetings I have about high-pressure horizontal hydraulic fracturing—which, David, if you'd called it that, would have made my life easier."

"Two percent's too high," he said.

"David," she said patiently, "two percent would be the lowest fracking tax in the country, hell, the lowest in the world, never mind the fact that France and most of Europe have banned fracking. So I think it's high time that you, your dad, your company, and all of your fracking friends accepted reality. We need fracking but we need to do it responsibly—a position that, as you can see, is making me unpopular with the crazies on the left and the crazies on the right—"

"Okay, let's play," I said to her. Cheating, I had put the tiles that would undo her on a rack and put this rack in front of her.

"Ha," she said, "that's beautiful. Well—crap—almost beautiful."

I played KING. I hadn't told Jill or anyone my plan, but she saw what was happening and did two things that, looking back on it, were completely contradictory. She told me to go easy on LaRue, to give the governor a chance, even as she raised David's phone to take a photograph.

"I will," I said.

"I'm serious. Try not to bite her head off."

"I don't know ... I mean I only have ..." All I had was my Scrabble plan—to make her play FRACKING, then tell her it was not a word, as if this would prove that the whole thing was a lie. No, in the end, it was David who really challenged her.

"Governor, do you remember the first time that we played?" he said.

"'Queueing,'" she said, shuddering. "The worst word I've ever seen."

"Do you remember where we were?"

"The Dark Suite at the Hilton. Why?"

"Do you remember the room number?"

"Yes, it was ... just a minute while ..." She played FRACKING and smiled as Jill took a photograph, which, when they ran it on the front page of the *Inky*, blurred my face and David's but showed FRACKING clearly.

49

I rode back to Hale in Thomasina's car and was hailed by her, by Mr. U, and by the entire school as a conquering hero, having won second place in the Scrabble tournament, and my game with LaRue having made the front page of the *Philadelphia Inquirer*.

My father was also incredibly proud of me. I didn't have the heart to tell him I'd cheated or that, more than FRACKING, David Dark brought her down. Yes, it was the final straw that made people wonder what else the governor didn't know — besides the fact that "fracking" was not actually a word — but I'd say there were two real death knells after me. The first was that the vice president who misspelled "potato" called to offer her his condolences, after which her name — like his — became synonymous with stupidity. The second was the news that suite 818 was the room where she used to stay in the Hilton — the room where she cooked up a way to "test water safely" — and that Suite Code 818 was now used by the Pennsylvania Department of Environmental Protection to designate water that should be tested for only some, not all, of the toxic metals and minerals that were burbling up in wells and being dumped in rivers and streams all over Pennsylvania. And this is the most amazing thing about my fracking odyssey. I had spent my entire life playing Scrabble and knew that, given a chance to play the governor, I could do *anything* — and it was this wild, irrational self-confidence that made me row around Dead Man's Curve and made the Feldkircher kid believe in me and give me the frackwater, which could have — should have — been enough to undo her. Mr. U — whose masterpiece was not a poem, exactly, more a bunch of documents that he thought would show the world that fracking was dangerous — would publish FRACK-ING as a poem in his next collection. A one-word poem whose title was "The Unwitting Confession of Linda King LaRue."

ACKNOWLEDGMENTS

```
      S    E D
      C    L
  B R O W N I N G
      T    S
      T  P A R K
         B   A
         E   P
         T   L
         H   A  L E X
             N
```